Omensfor

Cream Teas &
Crystal Balls

G Clatworthy

G Clatworthy
Swindon Book Fair 2024

ISBN: 978-1-915516-13-8

Cover design by Getcovers.

Foreword

A special thank you to my amazing typo hunters, grammar gurus, and plot pickers who got this story to where it is today. You are awesome!

If you want to support Gemma, you can find her on www.patreon.com/G_Clatworthy for exclusive first reads of new stories. You can also join her newsletter for a free short story based on one of the witches in the Omensford series and follow Gemma on www.instagram.com/gemmaclatworthy, www.facebook.com/gemmaclatworthy or join the Facebook reader's group Gemma's book wyrms.

Prologue

It was a bitter day. The sort you get in late autumn, as the weather shows glimpses of winter amidst bursts of leftover sunshine. No sun today though. No rain either. Just the cold, biting wind whipping at coats as eager shoppers hurried to their next purchases.

The young woman huddled in the doorway to get out of the wind and looked on vacantly. She used to play a game, wondering what was in each of the bulging bags held tight in pudgy hands. That had faded after two days on the streets. Sometimes her breath would catch as her eyes caught a flash of a haircut or coat that looked familiar. Her muscles bunched. She prepared to run before a more detailed look revealed that it was just an innocent passer-by. Not the monster she had fled.

If she still counted the days, she'd realise that today marked her thirty-first day on the streets. Over a month of sleeping rough, eating rougher. She scrounged food from bins at night and begged during the day. Sitting still and waiting for well-meaning pedestrians to drop coppers into

1

the empty cup in front of her. She had no mangy dog on a string lead to elicit sympathy and a day's takings was often less than a pound. So much for minimum wage. Still, she was lucky. She had escaped. And, sometimes, well-meaning people offered her food and a warm bed in a shelter, though it never lasted more than a couple of nights.

She spotted one of them now. A lady in her late forties with a kind face. Her life had been kind, mused the woman, her face was free from wrinkles or worry lines. She stood on six-inch stilettos as if she was above life's trials. She hadn't seen this woman before, but they were always the same. Always had the same look on their faces. They probably thought it was kindly concern, but she could spot the condescension behind their eyes and the hungering need to do good. It wouldn't matter what the 'good' was, just that they could be sure in their tidy little minds that good had been done. And what more obvious good than to offer a hungry vagabond a meal? In her mind, she nicknamed this one 'Stilettos'.

"Hello dear, you must be freezing."

The homeless woman made a noise in the back of her throat and kept her eyes forward, watching the do-gooder from the corner of her eyes. Stilettos wore a fitted coat that hid her body from neck to knees, but her hands were bare, open to the driving wind. She had probably never needed to consider wrapping up warm against frostbite in her entire easy life. The homeless woman curled her own hands, digging them deeper into her armpits for warmth.

"Such a pretty girl. You must have a sad story."

The woman gnawed her bottom lip and kept quiet.

"A man?" Stilettos guessed. The homeless woman looked up sharply before remembering her first rule: never make eye contact. She moved her gaze to a shop window across the shopping precinct. It showed a mannequin family dressed in matching argyle jumpers. The lady sighed dramatically. "It's always a man. Why don't you come with me, and we'll find you something to eat?"

The homeless woman decided she didn't like this well-meaning lady, but she wasn't stupid enough to turn down the offer of free food. She would take everything she could get, then disappear, just as she had done countless times in the past month, instinctively knowing that she would get less help the grimier and more wasted she became as she spent longer on the streets. She grunted and got to her feet, wincing a little. Her legs had gone to sleep from hours sat cross-legged on a cold, concrete floor.

"Good girl." Stilettos took her by the elbow and steered her through the crowded streets to an alley. The vagabond looked about nervously, her gaze darting around the street. This wasn't the usual shelter. Stiletto's held her fast, making sure her charge couldn't escape. She prepared to run, then they were through the alley and back onto a main thoroughfare. Her shoulders relaxed a little.

The older woman walked along confidently until they came to a hotel entrance. The do-gooder strode confidently across the marble floor and into a lift. As the lift rose, the homeless woman shifted from foot to foot. She was either in luck or in deep trouble. She risked a glance at her benefactor. The woman noticed and gave her a wide smile, her lips shining red.

"You really are a pretty thing, aren't you?"

She let them both into a large, plush bedroom with a credit card sized room key. The young woman paused. She had been in rooms like this before, when her boyfriend had been romantic instead of cruel and controlling. No one brought someone to a hotel room without wanting something in return. Her grey eyes sought a weapon.

"Now, why don't you get showered, and I'll order room service? What do you like?"

The homeless woman twisted under the guileless gaze. Maybe she was wrong. She eyed the exit and the bathroom door, gaping between them like a simpleton. Gnawing hunger, the sort that grinds in your gut, made her stay. Maybe she could get some food and run. The door was unlocked.

"Burger," she mumbled.

"Lovely. I've left some clothes for you in the bathroom. You can leave yours on the floor and I'll have them washed." The do-gooder sensed her hesitation. "Go on, scoot. I'll order food."

The homeless woman watched as the other picked up the phone and spoke to someone on the other end. Stilettos made a shooing motion with her hand. Reluctantly, the vagabond entered the bathroom.

4

Once inside, she locked the door. She took in the room. White and clean, with fluffy towels stacked on a glass shelf. No windows. No chance of escape here. She stripped quickly. Get this over with. Eat. Run. She ran the shower and got in, intending to get out quickly but the luxury of hot, running water stopped her from leaving. She used two entire bottles of each of the hotel's branded shampoo, conditioner, and bath gel to get clean, washing away thirty-one nights sleeping rough. The temptation of a hot bath pulled at her, a comfort unknown on the streets, but the smell of food wafted over the fragrant floral scent of the bath set. She dressed quickly, struggling with the zip on the fitted dress that hung on the back of the door. She paused to look in the mirror before she left the sanctuary of the bathroom.

Grey eyes stared back at her, surrounded by unblemished skin. She remembered what it was to be human and not ignored. Something near the sink caught her eye. A razor. She grabbed it and held it behind her back. A weapon. Just in case. No such thing as a free meal. Or a free hotel room. She opened the door and stepped back into the room.

Stilettos sat next to the room service trolley. She smiled. The homeless woman stalked over, sat down and with her free hand, began shovelling food into her mouth. The older lady left and went to the bathroom. She retrieved the grimy clothes and delicately bagged them up in silence. Through glimpses from under her long hair, the young woman thought she looked predatory, watching over a prisoner enjoying a last meal. She stuffed the last French fry into her mouth and stood.

"Going so soon?"

The young woman nodded, edging towards the door.

"But you haven't had dessert." Stilettos lifted a silver tray holding a thick slice of chocolate cake.

The vagabond shook her head, certain now that this was a trap.

"You haven't even told me your name." That same benign smile as Stilettos stood and walked forward, placing one foot in front of the other as though she was on a runway. A thought crossed the homeless woman's mind that she had seen the same smile before, on a cat before it devoured a rat in one of the alleyways where she sometimes slept.

She waved the razor in front of her, backing towards the door. Stilettos laughed. She raised her hands. Light pulsed, coming from her palms. The vagabond backed away, tripping over her own feet as she tried to get to the door. The older woman chanted and the younger one stopped moving. She lay on the floor, her face frozen in an 'o' of surprise, or maybe it was horror.

"There now. That wasn't so hard, was it?"

More chanting. The young woman's eyes darted around helplessly in her frozen body.

The older woman bent down and gripped the youthful face with her slender fingers. "Are you sure you don't want to tell me your name before you die?"

She tried to speak. To scream. But nothing came out. She wanted to say her name: Polly. Nothing. A tear spilled out of one grey eye and rolled down her frozen cheek. With a look

6

of interest tinged with enjoyment, the do-gooder completed her chant. Polly floated above the hotel room. From her vantage point near the ceiling, she watched with horror as her body stood, smoothed down the neat dress and stepped over the prone form of the older lady.

Her body lifted one arm and sniffed under her armpit. Her face crinkled into a grimace. "Still stinks," she heard herself proclaim. Humming, Polly's body stepped back into the bathroom. Polly shouted out, but no one heard. She tried to get back to her body but instead a force pulled her backwards, gently but insistently, like a small tug on her soul. Gradually, as if a camera moved out of focus, the room faded and then was gone.

Chapter 1

"Have you seen Neville's cock?"

Fi stopped dead, one foot across the threshold of her mother's house and her arms full of shopping bags. Why on earth was her mum talking about her brother-in-law's...nope she didn't even want to think the word.

"What?"

"Pardon. Not 'what'. I raised you better than that. Now, Neville's cock. It escaped by the village green; I thought you might have seen it while you were shopping."

"What do you mean it escaped?" Had her sister's husband finally gone mad and started flashing the local corner shop clients? He'd always seemed a bit odd to Fi. He enjoyed filling out tax returns, for goodness' sake.

"I mean it got out of the garden along with two of the hens. Last I heard, they were pecking at some breadcrumbs on the high street."

Fi's brain finally caught up with the conversation. "You mean Cluck Norris? Why didn't you just say so?"

"I don't know how I could have been any clearer. Anyway, I told Agatha that you'd help catch them. She's at work, and Neville's away on that accounting course."

"Why me?"

Nell gave Fi a look. "Oh, I'm sorry, do you have something better to do with your time?"

"Well, I…"

Fi's shoulders slumped. She wasn't going to win this argument. For some reason, playing on computer games all day wasn't considered a good use of time or a satisfactory method of processing trauma in her mother's book. "Alright, let me put the shopping down and I'll go."

"Excellent. Oh, and you can pop into Effie's café while you're in town. I said you'd show her how to use the till again."

Fi gritted her teeth. Effie was lovely, but the ninety-year-old had insisted on installing an inventory management system she had no idea how to use and now she called up her friend Nell almost every day asking for Fi's help with the technology. And her mother cheerfully volunteered her, knowing she still hadn't found a job and assuming that keeping busy would stop Fi from sinking back into lethargy and self-loathing after her power had destroyed a witch last year.

The witch had been a murderer and trying to kill her at the time, but it was still a traumatic memory for Fi. One that snuck up on her if she didn't keep herself occupied in the day, causing shivers and sweats…and at night…well, then

9

there was little escape from her own mind and the eternal replays of that day.

Fi sighed, dumped the bags of shopping on the wooden side in her mum's large kitchen, snagged a can of diet cola and headed straight back out. Behind her, she heard Nell's gripes about buying the wrong tins of beans.

"They were all out of the branded ones," Fi shot back as she closed the door. Getting the last word in was a small, petty victory to be sure, and one Fi would likely pay for later in some other small way, but honestly, sometimes her mother was too much of a stickler. She hoped that Nell didn't call up the local shop to complain because then she'd realise that the preferred beans were actually in stock, and Fi would definitely be in trouble. With a satisfied chuckle, Fi headed back into Omensford centre.

It didn't take her long to find the cockerel. Cluck Norris strutted down the High Street, blocking cars as people tried to go about their day. Any time a driver beeped their horn at the oversized chicken, the cockerel took it as a challenge and began a crow off. He lifted his beak to the sky and let out an almighty cock-a-doodle-doo. Fi jammed her hands over her ears and headed towards the offending bird.

"Sorry, yeah I know, yep, I'll just..." She manoeuvred herself through the small crowd that had gathered with their phones out to watch the car versus rooster show down until she was at the edge of the road.

Cluck Norris eyed her checked shirt with the malevolent eyes of a creature that knew it was descended from dinosaurs and tilted his head to one side.

"Here chick, chick," Fi tried.

Being a crowd of locals in a small town, the people gathered around immediately began to offer advice, despite having no expertise in chicken wrangling.

"What you want to do is to get down low, then it won't think you're a threat and you can get close to it."

"No, the best thing is to circle round it and get it from behind."

"Pretend you've got some corn, then he'll come right to you, he will."

Fi ignored the collective advice and edged closer. The cockerel let out another almighty crow and set off down the road.

"Oh, piss it." Fi set off at a run after the speedy bird as it raced away. The locals cheered her on as she chased the cockerel down.

"What do you suppose they call a group of chickens, then?"

"A fustercluck, I reckon, if they're anything like that one. Go on then, girl!"

Fi leapt towards the wayward rooster. Her fingers closed on one of his tail feathers. Cluck Norris let out a surprised cluck and put on another burst of speed before darting under a car.

"Ooo, you nearly had him then!" Sita shouted encouragingly from behind her phone, angling her camera better to capture the action.

Fi spotted Liv at the front of the crowd, laughing silently and fiercely. Tears of mirth ran down her perfect cheeks.

"I don't suppose you could dream walk him out of there?"

"Sorry," Liv gasped, wiping a tear from her face. "That's not how it works, they have to be asleep. And I'm not sure my dream powers work on chickens."

Fi swore. "Can you send him to sleep?"

The sleep therapist wiggled her fingers. "Sorry, it's a chicken. I'm not even sure it has a subconscious. If it was a person, I might be able to help." She checked her watch. "And I'd better go, I've got a patient in fifteen minutes."

"And patients won't wait?"

"A therapist's work is never done." Liv walked away, chortling, her short hair bobbing in time with her walk.

Fi brushed her white hair out of her eyes and lowered herself so she could peer under the four by four that Cluck was hiding under. She bit her lip as she thought. If only this was as easy as competing in first person shooters online. Her fingers twitched.

She could use her power. The electricity beneath her skin prickled to the surface in anticipation. She clenched her fist. Nope. That might fry the damn chicken. She clamped her power back down. It was too dangerous. And much as she was currently cursing the cockerel, she didn't think her sister would appreciate an electrified rooster.

"OK you lot, I need some help. We're going to surround the car so it can't escape."

"'Ere, I haven't got all day to be waiting round a car, love."

Fi stared down one of her neighbours before sighing. "Alright, you surround the car. I'm going to go under it and get the damn chicken."

The crowd moved around the large vehicle, blocking off more of the road. Drivers had long since given up on actually getting anywhere and joined the blockade, eager to hurry this along. Fi thanked the goddess that the car was far enough off the floor that she could wiggle under it. She flattened herself against the uneven road surface and inched her way underneath.

Cluck eyed her warily and immediately sprinted for the other side of the car. Seeing all the feet blocking his escape, he tucked himself close to one of the tyres and stared at the tech witch. Fi cursed as her bottom scraped along the chassis. The cockerel sensed it was cornered and made a last dash for freedom.

Fi propelled herself forward on instinct. Her hands closed around the large bird at the same time as her head connected loudly with the metal underside of the car. With another curse, she worked her way out from under the car while the chicken fought her all the way.

When she finally freed herself, the small crowd let out a tremendous cheer. Fi allowed herself a small smile before Cluck pecked her hand viciously.

"Ouch! You're going to end up fried if you don't behave!" she admonished the rooster, adjusting her grip so her hand was less of a target.

A polite cough sounded behind her. She turned and came face to face with a well-muscled chest in a tight t-shirt. She looked up and up into the deep brown eyes of Mortimer De'ath. Her mouth dried up. His eyes crinkled in amusement.

"I wonder if you'd be so good as to tell me what exactly you were doing under my car?"

Chapter 2

Dammit. Of course, it had to be his car.

"Er, I was just catching a cock, I mean, chicken." Fi thrust the offending rooster forward to prove a point.

"I see. It looks like he put up a fight." Mort gestured to the scratches and cuts on Fi's hands. "Would you like me to take a look at that?" Fi hesitated. "I am a doctor, after all."

Fi was about to reply that she was perfectly fine, but Mort's mastiff chose that moment to bark loudly at the cockerel, which startled Cluck. The rooster pecked Fi on the boob. She swore loudly and power instinctively crackled to her fingertips. The chicken let out a squawk of surprise at the small electric shock that rippled through it, sending its feathers sticking up. A faint smell of cooked chicken filled the air. Oops. She tamped her power back inside. She had to keep control.

"Of course she needs someone to check her out, bring her in here." Effie's voice carried across the crowd. "What are you lot doing standing around gawping? Show's over, clear off!"

Mort put his hand on the small of Fi's back and guided her to the café-cum-magic shop on the Omensford high street. Fi scowled down at Cluck as she allowed herself to be led away. Her sister and her chickens had a lot to answer for.

Once inside the familiar café, Effie gestured to a small table at the back and scuttled off to one of her back rooms. Fi took a seat at a small table next to a display of dreamcatchers. Effie ran the only independent café and witchy knick-knack shop in Omensford.

Effie returned moments later with a dog biscuit for the mastiff, a dusty first aid kit in a green box, and a wire-framed crate large enough for a small dog. It was just big enough for the fat cockerel. Cluck was still dazed from the electric shock and Fi got him into the crate with no more trouble. The dog settled down under the table, happily drooling as he devoured the bone-shaped biscuit.

"There now, I'll go get the rascally rooster some food and water."

"You've got chicken feed here?"

"Well, I'm sure I've got something. All you young people are vegan nowadays, so I've got a lot of grains in. Now as for me, I like a good steak and a block of cheese, so I couldn't go vegan."

Fi didn't know how to answer that, and Effie headed behind the small counter in the café to search for seeds.

"Let me look at that scratch."

16

"Huh?" Now the cockerel was safely under lock and key, well, bolted in a crate anyway, Fi tried to forget about the shenanigans under the car.

"The scratch, on your arm."

"Right, yeah." She made the mistake of meeting the doctor's eyes as she held out her arm for him to look at. She held her breath. The first time they had touched hands, her power had shocked them both. Fortunately, she was expecting the contact this time and kept her electricity under control. He smiled at her. She risked a smile back. Was he remembering the first time they met at the Halloween Fête too?

"Sorry, this might sting a little." Mort rubbed a small, white wipe over the abrasion. Not reminiscing about their first meeting then.

"What? Ahh! Sonofa pickle," Fi changed her curse word at the last minute as a family of five came through the door. She forced herself to breathe through the pain.

"Sorry." He looked more amused than contrite.

"It's alright, I'll get you at play time." The familiar words she always used with her sister were out of her mouth before she had thought about it.

"I'd better watch out then." His voice was low as he leaned in. Fi's mouth was suddenly dry. She opened and closed it once, unsure what to say. He lifted one hand to the side of her face. She felt a slight moistness on the side of her head, followed by the stinging pain of antiseptic. She winced and drew away. Bloody doctors. "Let me put a plaster on that."

17

Fi shrugged but moved closer to him. There was a sort of warmth that seemed to come from him and a reassuring earthy smell that was somewhere between freshly cut grass and spicy cinnamon.

"If you want to get her top off, you can take her in the back," Effie called, her voice ringing through the café. The family all turned to look in their direction. Fi turned a bright shade of red.

"I'm fine, thanks."

"Come on, love, that cock got you right in the bosom. There's no shame in getting the good doctor to take a look."

The parents' curious looks turned to embarrassed horror as they wondered what sort of establishment they were in.

Fi's face now resembled a freshly ripened tomato in colour. "Really, I'm fine."

Mort tried and failed to keep a straight face. Fi wanted to be angry, but instead burst out laughing as the parents quickly got their coffees to go and steered their children back outside. Clearly, they hadn't expected this type of behaviour on their day trip to the Cotswolds.

"Well now, I'd offer you a drink, but I've got to prepare for a reading. You can do the honours can't you, love?" said Effie as she swanned into the back room.

Fi nodded and stood. "What'll you have?"

"Coffee please, milk and one sugar." Mort followed the witch to the counter. Fi busied herself making the drinks, working the familiar barista machine with practised ease. The smell of Effie's particular blend of coffee took her back to her time as a teenager. "You look like you know what you're doing."

Fi nodded, "I used to work here, and Effie doesn't believe in changing technology. This is the same coffee machine from when I was fifteen."

It was almost a rite of passage in Omensford for teenagers to work either in Effie's café or at the local corner shop as they tried to earn extra money for whatever it is that teenagers do with their spare cash. Probably spend it on alcohol or drugs. Or in Fi's case, spare parts to upgrade the computer she'd built herself.

"Vintage coffee. Delicious." Mort said as he sipped his latte.

"It's not as easy as it looks, you know."

"I've got an espresso machine at home; how different can it be?"

"Alright then hotshot, you try."

Mort stepped up to the challenge and surveyed the machine. It was a shiny silver contraption with dials and buttons. Any indication of what anything did had worn off a long time ago, rubbed away by the hands of dozens of young servers. Fi crossed her arms and smiled as Mort stared at the machine.

"What'll it be?"

Fi pretended to think for a moment. "I think I'll have a cappuccino, please."

Mort raised an eyebrow, as if he knew that she'd picked the difficult drink deliberately.

"So, the steam comes out here..." He touched the spout and Fi nodded. "But where do the beans go?"

Fi shook her head and pursed her lips, enjoying the playful interaction.

"Give me a clue."

She pointed and, after some trial and error he eventually found the bean grinder and managed to get some of the granules into one of the filters. The doctor tamped it down to a compact coffee cake and tried to connect the filter to the machine. He thought he had it and turned to find a cup. Behind him, the metal filter clanged as it fell from the fitting, hit the drip tray, and landed on the floor. Mort swore. Fi laughed.

"OK doc, why don't you let me show you?" Fi stepped forward and handed the abashed doctor the dirty filter cup before taking a clean one and starting afresh. In less than two minutes, she had a perfect cappuccino in her hands.

"So, what are you up to for the rest of the day?" Fi asked absentmindedly as she wiped down the machine ready for the next customers. Too late, she worried that she sounded like she was fishing for a date.

"Oh, I'm going to see Dad and probably take Rus for a walk. Do you want to come?"

"Er, thanks for the offer, but I'd better see Cluck gets back home and Effie needs someone to look after the café."

As if on cue, a small woman dressed entirely in black entered the shop. She glanced around furtively before sidling up to the counter. Fi tried not to snigger at the world's worst spy act as the lady lowered her sunglasses and leaned forward.

"I'm looking for Madame Mystérieuse."

Mort frowned, but Fi knew who she meant. "The lady will be out any minute now, I'm sure. She just had to, er, prepare for the reading."

The lady nodded and stood by the counter.

"Would you like to take a seat? I'm sure she'll be out any minute." Fi mentally crossed her fingers that this wasn't one of the times that Effie would decide to take half an hour to 'commune with the spirits' before she deigned to see a paying customer.

The small woman frowned slightly and pursed her lips. "Will she be very long, only I've waited a long time to see her and," she lowered her voice and looked pointedly at the witch, "it's a matter of some urgency."

"Er…" Fi had no idea how to respond to that. Luckily, at that moment, Effie swept back into the room. She had donned what Fi liked to think of as her show woman's outfit. The elderly lady was draped in a purple wrap dress that was covered with gold and silver generic occult symbols. A shimmering golden shawl hung around her bony shoulders, and she'd topped the outfit off with a purple turban that had an enormous peacock feather crest, which balanced precariously on top of her white hair.

She paused in the doorway with one arm raised and the other stretched behind her, with a dramatic flair. Fi hoped the customer didn't look down. The mysterious effect was somewhat spoiled by the carpet slippers that Effie insisted on wearing inside her shop.

"I am Madame Mystérieuse and I sense a presence," Effie drawled, her voice lower than usual as she fell into her persona.

"Yes, yes, that's me. I'm here for a reading." The customer stepped forward and offered her hand for Effie to shake. The elderly lady awkwardly grasped the top of the hand between her thumb and forefinger and shook it disdainfully, as if the spirits wouldn't permit a proper handshake. Fi rolled her eyes behind the customer's back. She'd seen it all before. Mort stared in astonishment at the act.

"Grace?"

The customer gasped. "Yes! That's my name!"

"The spirits are anxious to talk to you." A slight pause and a lift of one bony hand. "Come through to my seeing room and I shall gaze into the crystal ball."

"Yes! I have so many questions!"

"Excellent, but remember, the spirits move in mysterious ways. We cannot always understand them." With a theatrical wink to Fi and Mort, Effie led the woman away into a back room that Fi knew from experience was decorated to look like a stereotypical fortune teller's room, complete with velvet drapes and tablecloth. It didn't matter that the table underneath was from the finest Swedish flat pack furniture

22

shop this side of Swindon. The point was that it looked the part and was solid enough for the knocks that people expected to accompany a visitation from the spirits. The look of the thing was half the battle, as Effie would say.

"What was that about?" Mort was blinking as if he couldn't believe the display he'd just seen. To be fair, seeing a ninety-year-old balancing a turban on her head wasn't exactly an everyday occurrence for a doctor.

"Oh, that's just Effie getting into the spirit for a crystal ball reading."

"Is she always like that?"

"Not always. Not with anyone who actually knows anything about magic anyway, but the mundanes like a show."

"What sort of thing does she read?"

"Whatever she sees in the crystal ball, I suppose. I've never been able to get on with the things myself." Mort quirked an eyebrow at Fi and she felt that she had to elaborate. "I've always preferred computers."

He screwed up his face in confusion. "You commune with spirits on computers?"

"No! I don't really do that sort of magic..." Fi trailed off. Mort knew she was a witch of course; she'd seen him for a fake heart condition last year and he'd pulled up her medical records. But they hadn't really talked about magic before.

"What sort of magic do you do?"

Fi swallowed and shifted. The kind who hurts people bubbled to the front of her mind and she shifted uncomfortably. The genuine curiosity in his gaze made her want to answer him, but she wasn't at ease with her destructive brand of magic, and he'd never be able to understand how much she fought to keep it under control. She opened her mouth to give him some bland platitude about electricity when the shop bell above the door rang.

Fi was saved from answering by a group of customers pushing their way into the café. They all giggled as they ordered traditional English cream teas in American accents and sat down at a circular table near the window to wait. It looked like one of the coaches that provided tours of magical spots in the UK had arrived. Fi sighed and began brewing the tea. At least they hadn't asked for afternoon teas, so she didn't have to make the sandwiches.

"So, are you going to tell me what sort of magic you do?" Mort broke through her thoughts as she placed three scones on the plain white plates that Effie had in stock.

"It's a secret. If I told you, I'd have to kill you," Fi deadpanned as she spread a thick layer of strawberry jam onto the fluffy scones, ignoring his interest and deflecting any talk of her magic.

He leaned forward. "Maybe that's a risk I'm willing to take. And it should be cream first, by the way."

"Don't make me stab you with a creamy butter knife." Fi waved the knife in his direction as she added dollops of clotted cream on the scones. She placed everything on a tray

24

and headed over to the table where the Americans squealed with delight as she unloaded their order, and they immediately began taking pictures of the quaint teapots and raisin-filled scones.

Fi smiled, asked them if they needed anything else, and retreated quickly back to the safety of the counter. She pulled up the inventory list again with a sigh. It was a mess.

"So, what'll it take to get your secret?"

"Hmm?" Fi replied, still paying attention to the computer.

"How about dinner?"

"Sure, sure." What on earth had Effie been thinking when she'd filled this thing out?

Mort checked his watch and waved goodbye as he retrieved his dog from where it had started to snore beneath one of the small tables. "See you later then. I'll pick you up at half seven?"

"Yeah, bye," Fi waved goodbye, still staring at the screen. About thirty seconds later, her brain caught up with her mouth. Hang on. Had she just agreed to a date with Dr De'ath?

Chapter 3

Fi scowled and snorted. If only people were as easy to understand as computers. The bell distracted her again. A teenager entered. She was sporting a black floor length gypsy skirt, a black corset top and a leather jacket. Black, of course. Her hair was dyed to match her clothes and her chunky platform boots clunked on the old wooden floorboards.

"Can I help with anything?" Fi asked.

The teenager grunted. Fi took that as a no and watched as the girl perused the stock.

"Are you a real witch?" The girl's head snapped up.

"Er…"

"I want to curse someone to keep away from me. Is that possible?"

"I don't do curses, but there might be something…" Fi tried to look it up on Effie's inventory system, but the old lady had used some sort of code and Fi couldn't work out what was in stock. She frowned at the computer screen, trying to figure it out. "Sorry, I can't see anything here. Try with the herbs at the back of the shop. All the spells are over there."

The girl nodded and headed in the direction Fi had pointed out. Fi shook her head. What did a teenager need to curse someone for, anyway? Probably a teacher who had given her a bad grade. Fi snorted quietly at her own joke.

A lanky teenage boy came in next and started looking around at all the stock. Fi mentally shook herself away from the till system. She was meant to be serving.

"Can I help?"

The teenager gave her a look, mumbled something and headed for the gothic girl still perusing the shelves. Her eyes shifted over the array of crystals and fossils in a glass case.

Fi watched them out of the corner of her eye as they had a heated, but whispered exchange. She couldn't catch any of the words, but the girl looked annoyed, then refused to make eye contact with the boy. Fi hoped the pimpled teenager wasn't her boyfriend. He raised his voice as his frustration mounted and Fi's power prickled under her skin.

"Come on, it'll just be this one time."

It looked like he was trying to persuade her to do something. Fi could make a guess as to what that might be. She tapped her finger on the keyboard and decided to do something. Just as she stepped out behind the counter, the boy turned and stomped towards her. Fi summoned her power to her fingertips automatically, before she realised what she was doing. She shook her hands quickly, brushing the electricity away. He was a spotty boy, for goodness' sake, and she was too dangerous and too jumpy. The teenager stopped in front of her.

"I want to know about curses."

Fi frowned. "What sort of curses?"

"Like, protection curses. To protect stuff and that."

"Do you mean like a ward?"

"Yeah, to keep people away from fings. Like there must be somefing around this shop right? To protect it."

"OK, sure, there are spells that can do that. There's some pre-made herb bags that you can use to make a basic ward. We have," she checked the database, remembered it was indecipherable and instead relied on her experience working for Effie over fifteen years ago, "some over there."

"And if I wanted to get through them?"

"You want to break a ward?" Fi squinted at the customer.

The teenager shrugged.

"It would depend on the strength of the spell. There might be something that could conceal you, so the ward couldn't sense you."

"Yeah, that'd do."

Fi pointed him in the direction of the ready-made spells. They were mainly for show, and the magic imbued in them was so low as to be almost worthless. The real spells that Effie sometimes did were custom made and took time and energy. A pre-made bag of herbs with a handful of words

28

attached wouldn't do much for someone without magical abilities.

The teenager grabbed something from the shelf, stuck it in his pocket, and headed for the door. Fi coughed.

"You going to pay for that?"

"Er, yeah, yeah." He threw a fiver onto the wooden countertop and waited for his change. Fi wished him a good day as he left. He ignored the witch as he stomped out of the shop. His face screwed up into the sort of moody anger that seventeen-year-olds do so well. Fi breathed a sigh of relief. She really didn't enjoy dealing with people. Especially moody teenagers. She got back to the inventory system. It froze. She tried a few keys then turned it off and on again. Worst case was that Effie would lose the database and she, or rather, Fi would have to rebuild it from scratch. At least then it would be understandable and, the first chance she got, she would back it all up to the cloud.

As the machine powered down, the middle-aged lady in black stormed through the beaded curtain that separated the shop from the back room. She had to disentangle herself from a string of fuchsia beads that caught in her hair, which gave Effie a chance to catch up.

"The spirits have their ways, dearie."

"Spirits? Spirits! You're a fraud, you are. A bloody charlatan! You think you can charge people good money to tell them rubbish like that?! I'm going to report you to...to...trading standards!"

Effie looked sympathetic but her voice was strong as she replied, "I am only a conduit for the other realm. I can't control how the spirits choose to communicate."

"There's no way that's my fortune, and there's no way that Pat would have left me with nothing, so you're a liar."

"I understand it's a lot to take in, love. How about a cup of tea? On the house?"

"You're deluded, you old fraud. You just want the money. Tell me where it is!"

"I already told you, there is no money."

"You stupid old bat. You'll pass over before me and then we'll see whose fortune comes true!" With that, the woman put on her bug like sunglasses and swept through the door.

"Not one of your satisfied customers, then?"

Effie shrugged. "Doesn't look like it. Still, at least she paid upfront. Here you go, you can put it in the till."

"About your till."

"What about it?"

"I've had to reboot it; did you change the password?"

"No, I've kept it the same as when you set it up…"

"OK got it." Fi interrupted hastily before Effie could tell the entire shop what the password was. It was only the gothic girl, now sulking around the wand collection, but still.

"Well, if you ever forget it, I've written it out under that coaster."

Fi glanced down at the coaster. A fluffy black cat stared back at her. Words printed around the edge declared; 'You're the cat's meow!'.

"You really shouldn't keep your passwords next to the device they're for," Fi whispered.

"But I need it when I log on. I don't want to be traipsing over the shop looking for it." Effie frowned.

Fi pursed her lips together. How could she explain password security to someone who's first idea for a secure password when she'd been told it needed a capital letter and numbers had been Password123? Maybe she should try to set up a fingerprint login...

They were interrupted by the girl approaching the counter with a small crystal ball and stand held delicately in her hands.

"Good choice love, that'll help you commune with the spirits and see fortunes."

The girl's purple lips curved upwards in a smile. "It spoke to me."

Effie nodded sagely and wrapped the glass sphere in tissue paper. "Remember to keep it covered with a cloth whenever you're not using it."

"Ooo, is that so the spirits don't escape their realm and cause mischief?"

Effie scrunched up her face as she regarded her customer. "No, it's because if you leave it uncovered in the sun, it can cause fires."

The young girl blushed under her pale make-up. "Oh right, yeah, course," she mumbled as she tapped her card to the card reader.

"Do you want to join the newsletter?" Effie asked, thrusting a piece of paper at the unsuspecting girl. The goth scribbled down her contact details, grabbed the paper bag containing her purchase and practically ran out of the shop.

Fi took the paper and typed the details into the database. It had been her mother's idea for Effie to have a newsletter and it was Fi who had the job once a month of typing up whatever Effie wanted to say and sending it out to her dozen subscribers.

Fi spent another couple of hours trying to go through inventory with Effie. The older witch thought her item descriptions, based on a combination of Latin and Olde English names were perfectly reasonable and refused to change them, even after Fi pointed out that it would be easier for any new staff to understand if it was in regular English. In the end, she compromised by allowing Fi to add an extra column to the database with an English name. Fi gave up trying to explain that an item should really only be marked as 'in stock' when it was actually in stock rather than 'could be made if required when Effie was in the store'.

She rubbed her eyes, a headache starting to set in. "I think that's all I can do today, Effie. I'll back this up to the cloud and I can come back tomorrow and talk you through the ordering system again."

"That'd be lovely, dear, although I'm not sure why the cloud wants to know about what I've sold today. A fresh batch of scones would be nice when you come; I expect there'll be another busload tomorrow." The nonagenarian looked distracted.

"Everything alright?"

"Yes, yes, there's something in the air, is all. Something… oh, never mind. Off you go, now."

Fi grabbed the crate containing an irate Cluck and set off to see her sister.

Chapter 4

Sometime later, a sweaty Fi arrived at her sister's house. Agatha was just locking the back door as Fi approached the front garden gate.

"Thank goodness! I was just about to come and find you!"

"Well, you could have set off a bit sooner; this chicken is heavy as an ox. What are you feeding him?!"

"That's an eggs-ageration if ever I heard one." Agatha looked very pleased with herself at the poor pun.

"Eggs-cruciating, that's what you are."

"I thought it was eggs-cellent."

"Eggs-actly what I'd eggs-pect from you."

"You're eggs-traordinary!"

"Alright, let's stop with the egg puns. Help me with the gate, would you?" Fi smiled at the moment of sororal bonding. They were so different in almost every aspect of their lives, but a strange sense of humour cemented their relationship.

Agatha laughed and unlatched the gate before taking the disgruntled rooster from her sister. "I hope Cluck wasn't any bother. I can't think how he got out."

"He's a demon chicken who pecked my boob in front of Mort and if you cooked him tomorrow, I wouldn't be sorry."

"Hush! She didn't mean that Clucky. Let's get you back with the others."

Fi followed her sister around the back of the semi-detached house, where three other chickens were roaming on the small patch of lawn. If one were watching the chickens closely, one might notice that any time they got too close to the copious vegetable garden, they gently changed direction away from the seedlings and freshly dug earth.

"They haven't got past the wards then?"

"No, I strengthened them after their last escape. I don't know how he got out." Agatha opened the crate and watched as the large cockerel strutted out towards his hens. The female chickens ignored Cluck completely and continued to peck at the bird seed on the grass. Agatha smiled down fondly at them.

Fi was about to make a comment about devious cocks when her niece came running outside.

"Aunty Fi!"

"Bumble Bea! How's my favourite niece?"

"I'm your only niece!"

"Are you?" Fi put one finger on her chin as if she was thinking. "You must be my favourite then!" She picked up the giggling girl in a hug before putting her down again quickly. She was always slightly afraid that she might injure her sister's daughter if she held her for too long.

"Have you got a present for me?"

Fi screwed up her face. "Sorry kid, I brought your chicken back, though."

"Kylo missed him." Bea's face turned serious, and she flounced off to check on the chickens. Fi looked out at the small flock, still ignoring the cockerel. She had been allowed the honour of naming Kylo Hen, choosing a Star Wars reference that no one got. Her online friends had laughed when she had told them though.

"Hang on, did you say Mort was there?" Now that she was sure her precious chickens were safe, Agatha had replayed their earlier conversation in her mind. "How is the handsome doctor?"

"Aren't you a married woman?"

The nature witch shrugged. "Doesn't mean I haven't got eyes. He's better looking than Li." Agatha ignored Fi's wince as she mentioned her sister's ex. "So, did you speak to him?"

"Maybe."

"And?"

"And he had to look at my injuries from your devil chicken."

"Cluck did that?!" Agatha took in the scrape on Fi's arm and the plaster on her face with disbelief.

"No, that was the pavement while I was under the car–"

"What were you doing under a car?"

"Trying to rescue your bloody cockerel!"

"Alright, alright, sorry. But about the doctor..."

"Well, he made sure I was alright, and..." Fi grinned sheepishly. "He asked me out. Tonight."

Agatha squealed.

"Bloody hell, Aggy!"

"Sorry but I have to live my life vicariously through you, now I'm a staid married matron. So, where's he taking you?"

"No idea. Somewhere with food, I expect."

"You're not going to make the WWWI meeting tonight, then?"

Fi tapped a finger to her chin again. "Hmmm, go to the monthly meeting of the Witches', Wizards' and Warlocks' Institute or have some nice food with a man. Tough choice."

"I know, Mum's invited Sita to give a flower arranging demonstration."

"I'd say I'm sorry to miss that but…"

"Well, it's nice to see you get out there again, we were all a bit worried after Li left you…"

"Hang on, how do you know I didn't break it off with him? And who's we?"

"Never mind, it's just good to see you dating again. Now you'd better go and find something to wear."

Fi looked down at her slouchy jeans and converse trainers. "What's wrong with my outfit?"

Agatha laughed and said goodbye. Just as her sister rounded the gate, Agatha called out, "Oh and Fi, don't be too, you know."

"What?"

"Don't be too...you."

Chapter 5

Fi stomped out of her sister's garden with her hands in her pockets. Charming. Her own sister thought she wasn't good enough for love. She thought briefly about calling the whole thing off, but she wasn't one hundred percent sure it was a date. Maybe he had some pressing medical news to share. And even if it was a date, that might get her Mum off her back about finding a nice man. And she did like food.

She paused on the pavement. Her old house was on this road. A small cottage on the other side and further down the hill. Technically, it was still her house as she was paying the sizeable mortgage on the two-bedroomed cottage, but when she'd lost her job, she'd been forced to rent it out to get some money coming in. She strolled down the hill nonchalantly. She wasn't checking on her tenant. Nope, she was just a casual passer-by taking a walk. Near a place where she happened to have lived.

She slowed as she passed her front door, trying to discern from the painted wood and butter-coloured Cotswold stone what her tenant might be doing. From the paperwork, it was a quiet couple who had moved from London and were checking out the area before they committed to buying somewhere in the country. But you always had to watch the quiet ones. They could be drug dealers or anything. Surely it was her civic duty to knock on the door and check it out for herself. The door stared back at her. Daring her to approach.

"Penny for them."

Fi jumped.

Steve laughed. "You were away with the fairies!"

Fi touched her ear and made a sign to ward off any ill luck from mentioning the fae folk. "Just wondering about the tenants. I haven't met them yet."

Steve nodded sagely. "Well, I can tell you they've been having raves every night."

"Sorry, I'll go speak to them." Fi had one hand on the gate as Steve carried on.

"And they even invited us to an orgy last Friday."

Fi narrowed her eyes at her old neighbour. "I can go off people, you know."

"Come on, they're perfect neighbours. In bed by ten. No shenanigans. Glen is thinking of having them over to dinner."

"Are they supernatural, then?"

"I don't think so. We haven't seen any signs. Probably just a nice mundane couple who want to put down roots away from the big city. Either that or the thought of the WWWI Spring Social drew them here."

Fi winced. She'd forgotten about the social. Maybe she could find a way to get out of it this year. "Do they know you're...?"

Steve shrugged. "It's not exactly like I can drop it into the conversation. 'Hi, I'm Steve and this is Glen and by the way we're both werewolves so, if you hear any howling on the full moon, don't worry about it.' How well would that go down? We'll tell them if they need to know. What about you? Do they know they're renting off a witch?"

"I didn't exactly put it in the ad. But if they're ever late with the rent, I can always mention it."

"Threaten to curse them, you mean?"

"Well, if they're mundane, they might fall for it."

"How's Nell doing?"

"You know Mum. She wants to run everything in the village."

"Alright, I'd better go in, Glen wants these for the venison casserole." Steve brandished a brace of carrots. "Fancy staying for dinner?"

"I'd better get back. I've got to change."

"For the WWWI meeting?"

Since the local WWWI chapter had declared itself a diverse group, open to any magical being, the werewolves had been to every meeting religiously. The resident witches had welcomed them with open arms, especially since they brought chocolate biscuits or brownies with them and anyone who knows witches knows how easily they can be swayed by delicious baked goods.

"Actually, I won't be there."

"Oh?"

"I'm going out."

"Who is he?"

"Who said anything about a he?"

"You can't fool these werewolf ears; I heard the change in your voice. Who is he?"

"Can't I have any privacy?"

Steve shrugged. "If you want privacy, live in a city."

"I'll tell you tomorrow. If it goes well."

"Someone local then."

Fi mimed zipping her lips and waved as she headed back to Nell's house. Fi strode home in a better mood after her chat with the werewolf. The door of the large three-storeyed family home opened as soon as she put one foot on the step. Fi smiled and patted the doorframe in thanks as she passed through. She'd learned the hard way not to ignore the house. Several hours spent locked outside in the frosty night air by a house that is sulking because it hadn't been thanked is a lesson a child never forgets.

Fi pulled off her converse trainers and put them neatly in the shoe rack before turning into the kitchen to grab a snack. She spotted the small golden wyrm curled up in a basket stuffed with blankets by the large range cooker.

"Hey Cress."

I've told you before not to call me that!

"It's cute, like a nickname."

My name is Lady Cressida Charmington.

"That sounds like a weird game avatar."

The dragon-like creature eyed the witch. *Would you like me to add some more cuts to your arm?*

A spark of annoyance flittered in Fi's mind. She didn't question why she was annoyed and instead held her hands up in mock surrender, knowing that the wyrm would indeed lightly maul her with very little provocation. "Alright, alright, Cressida it is. Where were you earlier, anyway? I could have used your help rounding up a rogue rooster."

The small wyrm gave Fi a look that said even if she had been there earlier, she certainly wouldn't have helped capture a chicken.

"Well, I'm going out tonight so you can stay here or go with Mum to the WWWI meeting."

"What's that about the WWWI meeting? You are coming, aren't you?"

Fi shook her head. Honestly, it was as if just talking about the institute summoned its local Chairwoman. "No, I can't come. I'm meeting someone for dinner."

"Oh yes, Effie said you had a date."

Bloody small towns. "It's not really a date."

Nell raised one perfectly shaped eyebrow. "Hmmm. Well, I suppose you won't be wanting any food then? You might have told me earlier. I've made a roast."

"I thought Effie told you."

"I do like to hear things from my own daughter from time to time."

"Yes, Mum."

"How was Agatha?"

"Aggy's fine. Cock all in one piece and returned safely."

"There's no need to be vulgar. You can make a cup of tea before you get changed. I've got to call Sita to go over the arrangements for tonight."

"I think she knows what she's doing, Mum. She is a trained florist, and didn't she do the flowers for the Bowood House Christmas display last year?"

"Yes, but I want to be sure she's got enough ivy for everyone to make a wreath and I saw this fabulous display online that I think would be perfect for us all to attempt."

Fi rolled her eyes as her mum turned to look for her phone. She would have to apologise to Sita for introducing Nell to the online pin boards that were giving her even loftier aspirations for the local floral displays.

She made hot drinks, using the tea bags she kept in the cupboard, much to her mother's disgust, and making sure to throw the used bag in the compost. If she couldn't see the evidence, her mum couldn't often tell the difference between a brew made with tea leaves or tea bags. She did, however, pour Nell's drink into a china teacup and placed it on a saucer to avoid any comments about 'standards'. She poured her own cup of black coffee, with two sugars, into a large mug and took it to her bedroom.

The door swung open as she approached. "Thanks," she said aloud to the house. It was obviously in a good mood today, and she didn't want to accidentally offend the semi-sentient building.

She glanced down the hall to the guest rooms. There was no one here at the moment, but the Bed & Breakfast would have a least a couple of bookings over the Bank Holiday weekend. With all the nature witches in the protected magical village of Omensford, people were pretty much guaranteed great weather, and that was often enough of a draw for people who wanted a picture-perfect getaway for the long weekend. As always, her eyes lingered on the one door that never opened. No one knew for sure what had happened to her uncle, but he'd gone into his room one evening and never come out again. She shivered and stepped over the threshold into her own bedroom.

Nell hadn't changed Fi's room since she'd moved out, insisting that her children would always have a place in her home. Fi was almost upset she hadn't redecorated. Instead of staying in a plush guest room, she was sleeping on a single bed with a duvet covered in cartoon characters from the early nineties.

Not to mention the embarrassing posters that lined the walls. Fi grimaced. Why had she ever thought a succubus with oversized tits was cool? She'd have to get round to tearing them down now she was back home permanently. She was tempted to do it now, but her sister's words rang through her ears and Fi balled her fists and turned her attention away from scantily dressed gaming characters.

She didn't want to mess this up. She had to at least try. After all that was one of the reasons Li had left. He was sick of being the one who made all the effort. Fi snorted, annoyed that she was going down this road. It wasn't like he was perfect.

OK, on paper, he had been perfect... and if she was being honest... he had been pretty perfect in real life, too. Thank you dating algorithms. He had just wanted more from her than she had to give. And he hadn't given her any space. No, thank you. She needed her independence. If she wanted to spend all night playing some first person shooters online, she needed someone who could understand that.

Her eyes landed on her gaming computer. Maybe she had time for one quick round of Fortnite. Since she'd been home, she'd set up her gaming rig on her old desk alongside her trusty laptop; the only piece of electronics she hadn't blown up with her unpredictable magic. She ran her fingers along the keyboard. It was tempting.

Her cupboard doors flew open, and clothes started spilling out onto the floor.

"Alright, alright, I'm getting dressed!" Fi had no idea how the house knew what she needed, but when it was right, it was right. She picked through the pile of clothes and held up a few items against her body as she looked in the mirror. Why was fashion so hard?

She discounted the clothes she had left here when she'd moved out. Another thing to add the list of stuff to clear out, besides a cropped Hello Kitty top wasn't ironic when you were the wrong side of thirty-five. After what seemed like an age, she gave up and pulled on a black sweater dress over some leggings. She applied some lipstick, decided it was too bold, and spent another five minutes trying to remove it without smudging it around her mouth like some sort of clown mask. Her hair frizzed out as she stressed over the balance between making an effort and trying too hard. She had just tied her long mane into a ponytail when the doorbell sounded.

It took her a minute to place the sound because no one ever used the front door to the B&B. She glanced at the clock and realised it must be Mort. Fi swore and rushed out of her room, her only pair of high heels dangling from her fingers as she raced to open the door.

Chapter 6

"Sorry," she panted breathlessly after her short run down the stairs. "I'm not usually late."

She stopped talking. There was a young woman standing on the porch. Not the attractive doctor she was expecting.

"Oh, hello, actually I'm not expected, but I'm after a room if you've got one." The young woman paused and waited for Fi to reply. Fi's brain was still playing catch up at the unexpected visitor, so the woman carried on. "The sign says 'vacancy' so I thought it would be alright to just knock. But if you're full…"

"No, no, we're not. I'll just get my Mum; she runs the B&B. Mum!" she shouted. No answer. Great. "Er, welcome, by the way. I'm Fi. Can I take your bags?"

"No thanks." The lady pulled her small, wheeled suitcase closer towards her legs and stepped forward. Fi moved out of the way to let her in. As she stepped over the threshold, the front door started to close. Fi spotted it out of the corner of her eye and moved to hold it open. The young woman spotted the movement and turned sharp green eyes on the tech witch.

"Is something wrong?"

"No, not at all, it's just, well the house can be a little temperamental at times. But it would never harm a paying guest." Fi raised her voice a little at the last two words to make sure the house knew this was business.

"A real sentient witch's house?" The woman looked around as if she was appraising the building before she returned her attention to Fi. "How thrilling! I'm so glad I decided to stop here and check you had space."

Once the guest was safely inside, Fi stepped away from the door and led the way to the small desk where her Mum did all the bookings. The front door slammed behind them, and Fi grimaced at the house's temper tantrum. No doubt she would pay for that later. Fi placed her high heels on the polished desk, logged in and started to fill out the guest's details when she heard a familiar voice in the kitchen.

Mort was here. And he was talking to her mother. Unsupervised. A small pulse of nervous electrical power arced from Fi's fingertips into the computer. The screen flickered and went dead. Fi swore.

"Sorry about this, the computer's playing up. Can I take down your details and then I'll find Mum, I mean Nell, and she'll show you to your room."

An amused smile played around the guest's lips, and she repeated her name. Fi wrote it down as fast as she could.

"Great, great, and how long do you think you'll be staying for?"

"Oh, a week should be quite long enough I expect."

Fi noted that down, not really paying attention. "And can I ask what you're planning on doing while you're here? We've got a few pamphlets for local attractions and if you need any recommendations on places to eat out, the local pub's great."

"Thank you, but I'm here for family not for sightseeing."

"Right, right, OK well I've got everything I need, I think. I'll just go find Mum." Fi grabbed her shoes and rushed to the kitchen. Mort sat at the long kitchen table with a cup of tea in front of him and her mother was actually smiling as they discussed the weather. Nell never looked this relaxed with anyone. Not even her daughters. Maybe especially not with her daughters. Fi narrowed her eyes at the scene before remembering why she was here.

"Mum, there's a guest here."

"Well, why didn't you say so, dear? Ah, you must be the guest."

Fi turned to see the young woman in the doorway behind her. "Yes, this is her. Miss…" Fi looked down at the piece of paper in her hand where she'd scrawled the name. Her writing was illegible.

The young woman smiled and held her hand out to Nell. "Adriana Harrington."

"Harrington?" Nell asked, taking the proffered hand and shaking it vigorously. "I don't suppose you're related to Ophelia Harrington?"

"Actually, I'm here to see her. She's my great aunt!"

Fi frowned, trying to place the name. "Who's Ophelia Harrington?"

"Effie, of course. I'm seeing her tonight as it happens. I'll mention you."

"Oh, do you mind if I come with you? I'd so love to see her. I was going to try to find her tomorrow. Apparently, she runs some sort of shop?" Somehow Adriana made it sound like she was looking down on the business.

"Yes, the local café. She does really well." Fi bristled at the slight to Effie and over exaggerated the café's success.

"Of course, you can come with me, the WWWI is always happy to welcome new members." Nell glared at her daughter's poor manners.

Adriana blanched at the mention of the WWWI. Fi wondered if she'd had experience with a local branch. "Perhaps I should wait and see her tomorrow."

"Nonsense, it's no trouble at all. Fi can show you to your room and then we'll be off." Nell sensed Fi's hesitation and shooed her out with the universal gesture of two hands motioning towards the door. "Go on, the doctor and I are having a lovely chat."

Fi looked from her mother to Mort, who grinned back at her. She swore inside her head and hurried up the stairs. Adriana followed elegantly behind her, perfectly at ease on her high-heeled shoes. Fi led the way to the guest section of the house, a series of spacious rooms. She unlocked the door of the one farthest from her own room and took a deep breath.

Showing a guest to a bedroom was always a surprise as the house redecorated its rooms to suit the personality of whoever stayed with them. Fi fervently hoped that Adriana didn't have any weird fetishes as she recalled the middle-aged couple in tweed who had been delighted to find a leather swing in their room last summer. Fi could still hear the creaks in her nightmares.

Fi opened the door and gestured for Adriana to step inside. The house picked the perfect individual décor for every person, offering Fi a glimpse into their lives. The young woman looked around, taking in the minimalist décor in black and shades of white. An art déco painting hung on the wall, providing the only spot of colour in the room. It reminded Fi of a fancy London hotel. She thought Adriana must enjoy luxury and maybe the 1920s.

"Very nice," Adriana murmured appreciatively as she crossed the threshold, drumming her fingers on the mirrored cabinet next to the door.

Fi stopped gawking at the decorations. "OK, I'll leave you to it then. Mum will let you know when she's ready to leave."

Fi handed over the key and hurried back downstairs. Mort and Nell still sat at the kitchen table. Mort stood when Fi entered the room.

"Thank you, Mrs Blair, now I really should get going if we're going to make our reservation."

"Of course. I'd better get ready for the WWWI meeting, anyway. See you later, Fi. Have fun on your date."

Fi blushed. She'd been trying to forget it was a date. She looked at the doctor. "Shall we go then?"

"Of course." He gestured to the back door, which was already open, letting in the unseasonably warm night air.

Fi led the way through the garden, focusing on keeping her balance in her stupid heeled shoes. Why hadn't she stuck with her usual converse trainers? She paused at the gate. "Where are we going?"

Mort smiled and led her to his four by four. "I thought we'd go somewhere outside Omensford if that's alright. It's such a small village, I wanted us to go somewhere where we could talk."

Fi nodded as he opened the passenger door, and she hopped into the large car.

"Nice car."

It was comfortable inside, obviously not a utilitarian vehicle. That made sense. He was a doctor after all. Fi turned her mind away from what he might be earning, it only heightened the sting that she was still unemployed, and her best prospect so far was the local café.

"Thanks, it gets me from a to b. The salesperson talked me into the premium paint job though, so now I'm scared every time I drive down a country lane that I'll scratch it."

"No dog tonight?" Fi attempted a joke as Mort climbed in behind the steering wheel and started the engine.

He turned towards her with a devastating smile. "He scratches the leather and besides, tonight's just for the two of us."

Chapter 7

Fi swallowed, her mouth full of cotton wool at the promise in his voice. She tapped her fingers nervously against her thigh and looked out of the window in the fading daylight as Mort drove. She recognised the familiar countryside as he wound the car through narrow roads and carefully over cattlegrids on the road to Magewell. She forced herself to breathe normally and pushed away the magic that she could feel trying to surface.

There was nothing to worry about. No rogue, murderous witches here anymore. Her fingers tapped against her thighs as she gazed out of the window. It was just another small village in the Cotswolds that had a magical community. Nothing unusual about that. But her shoulders still tensed as the doctor found a parking space on the high street. He walked round to open her door while she struggled with the seatbelt, her nerves making her clumsier than usual.

Mort offered her his hand, and she took it without thinking. As their palms connected, a small spark of electricity arced between them, and Fi yanked her hand back.

Mort rubbed his hand thoughtfully and offered her his arm instead. "That's the second time that's happened."

"What?"

"The first time we met, in the coffee tent at the Halloween Fete, we had the same static electricity. There must be sparks between us," he joked.

"Yeah," Fi replied weakly, with a small laugh.

Mort let it go and walked them towards an Indian with a purple sign out front declaring this was: The Maharajah. He opened the door and Fi walked in, maybe she could get used to being treated like a lady. A smiling host in a crisp white shirt under a purple embroidered waistcoat, greeted them and led them past a family already tucking into starters, to a booth that Mort had reserved. As he introduced himself as Sanjeev, he handed them menus and took their drinks order, then deftly recited the specials before retreating to get their beverages.

Fi stared down at the menu, not really seeing the exotic dishes. A gold star caught her eye above a small statement proclaiming The Maharajah was the 'best restaurant in the South West two years in a row'. She vaguely remembered reading something about this restaurant winning an award in the local paper. The waiter arrived with their drinks and a plate of poppadoms and set them on the table with a flourish.

"Cheers." Mort raised his glass of chilled lager.

Fi raised her own half pint of lager, mixed with a dash of lime, as she was having a curry, and chinked it against his. "Cheers."

The doctor smiled and selected a poppadom before dipping it into the lime pickle. "Have you decided what you're having? The jalfrezi they do here is excellent."

"Er, I thought I might have the biryani." Fi relaxed as they slipped into small talk, some of the tension falling from her shoulders as she contemplated the menu.

"Great choice."

Fi broke her own poppadom into smaller pieces before spooning one of the sauces onto it. She wasn't paying attention and only realised her mistake as her mouth tingled then burned. She had lathered the crisp-like starter with spicy lime pickle instead of sweet mango chutney. Fi quickly grabbed her drink and took a large mouthful. Unfortunately, she mistimed her gulp and ended up coughing as she desperately tried to breathe normally again.

"Are you alright?" Mort stood, preparing to give her the Heimlich manoeuvre.

Fi waved him away. "Fine, just went down the wrong way," she gasped out as she tried a smaller sip of her lager. Now she couldn't even drink properly. He must think she was an idiot. The family sitting in the window stopped eating their onion bhajis and were watching the show with interest.

Fi nearly started spluttering again. The server came back, full of concern, and Fi reassured them both that she was perfectly fine.

One of the children piped up. "Is that lady dying?"

"No dear, her drink just went down the wrong way."

"How can a drink go down wrong?" The boy's brow creased as he tried to understand.

"Hush now, eat your chicken wings."

The boy started trying to drink his lemonade backwards, much to his parents' dismay and amusement.

"I think we're ready to order." Mort saved Fi from any more embarrassment by redirecting the waiter's attention. He produced a pad of paper from a pocket and wrote down their orders before disappearing to the kitchen.

Fi fiddled with her cutlery some more before asking the question that was on her mind, "So your surname's De'ath..." Mort waited patiently for the inevitable question, "...and you're called Mort..."

"It's short for Mortimer."

"Right, right," Fi replied hastily. She'd known that. She rearranged her serviette compulsively.

Mort sighed. "My Dad has a very strange sense of humour. It's why he chose the dog's name, too."

Fi frowned slightly as she tried to remember what the dog was called. "Rus?"

"Yeah, it's short for Cerberus."

Fi snorted. "Really?"

Mort nodded.

"Wow, you weren't joking about your dad's sense of humour."

"I know right, I'd feel sorry for myself, but Dad's name is even worse..."

Fi waited expectantly and took a sip of her lager.

"...Hades."

Fi coughed cold beer all down her front before trying to recover herself.

Mort shrugged. "I guess you could say it runs in the family."

"At least you're not called 'Sutton'."

The doctor frowned.

"As in Sutton Death...sudden death..." Nervous again, she went back to picking at the napkin. Not everyone appreciated her strange sense of humour.

Mort's deep laugh carried across the restaurant, causing the family to turn their way again. Fi smiled too; she was starting to enjoy herself.

"So, you've heard about my family. Tell me about yours. What magic powers run in the Blair family?"

Fi opened her mouth just as the restaurant owner himself came out to oversee the serving. "Lovely to see you again, sir!"

"Good to see you too, Rahul."

"Are you enjoying everything?"

"Yes, thanks."

"Can I get you a drink, sir, madam?"

"I'm fine, thanks."

"I insist, whiskey? And Baileys for the lady?" Rahul whisked away and poured the drinks himself before returning and placing two square glasses on the table along with a single red rose. "A beautiful flower for a beautiful lady." He handed it to her with a flick of his wrist and a winning smile before he disappeared out back.

"I didn't know you knew the owner." Fi whispered as she tucked into her biryani, savouring the subtle spices. She was annoyed at the attention, uncomfortable with the compliment and she didn't even like the coffee flavoured liqueur. She preferred her coffee hot and black, with two sugars.

"I don't, not really. Dad knows him better; he was Rahul's doctor for years. I just sort of grew up coming here."

"How is your dad?" Fi thought of the old doctor. He'd been looking elderly since she was a teenager, but he'd always been there. A reassuring voice of reason that dispensed antibiotics and painkillers and had told her in no uncertain terms that the repetitive strain injury she suffered in her wrists was a result of too much time hunched over a computer screen.

"He's muddling along. He's finally decided to retire after his health scare last year and I've decided I'm going to take on his practice."

"Oh." Fi felt a warm feeling spread from her stomach through her body. She took another sip of lager, unsure what to say. It wasn't the most articulate response, but she was glad that he had decided to stay in Omensford.

Mort nodded. "It's a bit different to my previous practice, smaller but being back here last year, well it brought up some memories, and Dad and I had a long talk, and it turns out I quite enjoy the quiet village life."

"Just make sure you avoid my mum if you want your life to stay quiet."

"Oh?" Mort raised one dark eyebrow.

"She'll have you on the Spring Social organising committee before you know it."

"Ah." He shifted uncomfortably.

Fi laughed, remembering Nell and Mort had had a few minutes alone together earlier that evening. "She already got you to agree to it, didn't she?"

Mort smiled sheepishly before saying doubtfully, "Maybe it won't be too bad."

Fi snorted and shook her head. "Poor, innocent Mort, how little you know."

"Sounds like I need someone who knows their way around these things to help me out…"

"A guide, you mean?"

"Someone who's on the inside track with the organisers…"

Fi raised an eyebrow at the doctor, enjoying the banter. "I don't know, family loyalty counts for a lot."

"Please. I'll be in your debt. I'll do anything."

61

She smiled slowly and tapped one finger against her jaw. "That's a lot of power to give me."

He leaned forward and licked his lips. "Anything you like."

Fi leaned back and raised her glass. "Alright, but I'm holding you to that."

Chapter 8

Meanwhile, at the Omensford WWWI meeting...

Agatha was worried. Her mother made a point of being punctual for everything in life, and by punctual that meant she arrived wherever she was going within exactly thirty seconds of when she was meant to be there.

For the sacred Witches', Wizards' and Warlocks' Institute meetings, however, she was always early. All the better to make sure things were arranged as she liked them, and, of course, it gave her the opportunity to smile benignly at the members as they arrived, ever so slightly asserting her superiority over the others and making them feel like they were late.

But today, she was late and Agatha had felt unable to comment when someone set the chairs up in small groups of four or five rather than the usual semi-circle, and the rectangular table that usually presided over the meeting was set to one side.

When her mother arrived, one minute after the prescribed start of the meeting and with a younger woman in tow, it was obvious that she was irked.

The WWWI members chatted to each other over cups of tea and homemade fairy cakes while Sita unloaded various plants onto the little wooden tables that were usually used for the bridge club.

Agatha started to walk over to her mother, standing by the door, taking in the unruly scene, but Nell held up a slender hand to stop her. She watched her mother straighten her spine, step forward and clap her hands together.

"It's so lovely to see everyone this evening, and of course I want to thank Sita for agreeing to teach us all some flower arranging. I have seen her bouquets, and I have high hopes for this evening and for all of you."

"Thank you, now…" Sita started.

"Before we start, there are some matters of business to attend to," Nell cut over Sita smoothly. "Firstly, I want to make sure that everyone knows about the Spring Social. I've scheduled it for the bank holiday weekend for maximum attendance and donations for the raffle are welcome."

"I could do a reading!"

"Thank you, Effie, I'll certainly bear that in mind."

"You're welcome," Effie mumbled around a mouthful of biscuit. She took out a pad of paper to record the minutes of the meeting and knocked Sita's arm, sending the cream flowers she had been holding fluttering to the ground.

"I'm so sorry, dear. Cake?" Effie shoved the box of iced cakes in front of the shaken woman. "No? They're really good. Oh, well, your loss."

"If we're quite done." Nell brushed over the commotion as Sita bent to gather the blooms that now covered the hall's scratched wooden floor. "I've invited the other local WWWI branches to the social, of course. We have to show solidarity and we'll split any funds raised between the Omensford, Magewell and St Columba branches. I also wanted to note that in rather a coup, I've managed to get a special DJ - Jeremy Vinyl–"

"Oooo, I love his radio programme. I can't wait to meet him. Such a nice fella."

"Did you hear his show the other day? They were talking about vampire devices."

"Why would a vampire need vices?"

Nell sighed and took back control of the meeting before it continued down the rabbit hole. "No, not Jeremy Vine. Jeremy Vinyl; he's a local DJ who's promised us a 'rocking set'." Nell inserted the inverted commas with practised ease. "Alongside the Hoedown Hobgoblins, of course." And finally, I wanted to introduce our newest member for tonight...Miss Adriana Harrington. You can pay the subscription at the end of the night. Now, I'll hand over to Sita Kumar for her much-anticipated flower arranging display."

Effie dropped her pen and looked up sharply. Agatha rushed to hand it back to the secretary as the young woman gave her a small smile and waved her hand. The nonagenarian ignored Agatha, shuffled over, and squinted at the newcomer.

"Who are you supposed to be?"

Agatha started in surprise at Effie's rude question and placed the pen back on the table, but Adriana just smiled back.

"I'm not surprised you don't recognise me, Ophelia. I'm your great niece." She held out her hands wide as if to give her great aunt a hug.

Effie snorted. "Hells you are. What are you doing here?"

Adriana's expression turned sad. "I'm not surprised you don't recognise me. I know you and my…grandmother weren't close, but I wanted to seek you out. My only living relative."

"Huh."

"I'd really like to spend some time with you," Adriana persisted.

Effie looked around the room, as if suddenly realising that the assembled supernaturals had paused their conversations to watch the exchange. She shifted her weight between her feet, before meeting the younger woman's eyes. "Not now."

"Of course, I'm excited to try flower arranging." Adriana's voice didn't sound too false as she smiled at the room. "I'll find you tomorrow."

Effie grunted and headed back to her seat.

"Are you alright?" Agatha reached out and placed a hand on Effie's arm. The old lady trembled in her chair.

"I jus' didn't expect to see her." Effie shook her head, causing her wispy hair to fall over her eyes. "I'll be alright."

With a nervous cough, Sita began her flower arranging display. She encouraged the WWWI members to follow along and the ladies and gentlemen were soon pressing stems into pre-soaked green foamy oasis sponge.

Partway through, just as Steve let out a giant sneeze after sniffing a lily, Effie got up to make some tea. Adriana got up and followed her out. Agatha made her way to the small kitchen too, ready to offer help, but she paused on the threshold as Effie turned on the young woman.

"Why are you here?" The elderly witch asked rudely.

Adriana leaned easily on the Formica kitchen surface as Effie placed tea bags into cups and boiled the limescale-laden kettle.

"Would you believe me if I said a cup of tea?"

"That's not what I meant, and you know it. Why have you sought me out after so many years? How did you find me?"

"It wasn't easy, I'll give you that. But one hears rumours. I didn't think you'd be so obvious about it, but you never were exactly subtle, were you?"

Steve's sneeze sounded through the partition wall.

"You're one to talk!"

"Temper, temper Ophelia."

"What do you want?"

"I think you know what I want."

Effie shook her head. "Well, you'll not get it."

"We'll see." She turned her head and caught Agatha hovering in the doorway. "Can we help you?"

"Er, hello, just thought I'd pop in to see if you wanted any help with the tea, and, er, get some tissues for Steve," Agatha nervously interjected. A loud sneeze carried into the room as if emphasising her words.

"Yes, well, I think I'll head back and get an early night. We've got a lot to discuss tomorrow, Aunt Ophelia."

Effie slammed a cup down hard on the countertop as Adriana wafted out of the poky kitchen and left the hall. Agatha stared. What on earth was going on? She had no more time to ruminate on the strange behaviour as another explosive atishoo sounded from the hall. She stepped forward to grab some kitchen roll for the sneezing werewolf and hurried out of the room.

Chapter 9

Fi was surprised to find she was smiling as Mort drove them home. She was tired but content and at peace. She watched the scenery flash by, made silver by the light of the gibbous moon. It was almost magical. Her smile turned wry at that and she shook her head at her own foolishness.

"Penny for them?"

"Hmm?"

"Your thoughts. You were shaking your head."

"Oh, I was just thinking the night was magical."

"I think it is." Mort's words held more meaning than she was comfortable with, and she stumbled to think of a reply. Instead, she stared back out of the tinted windows of the large car, glad to see the Omensford sign flash by. Mort kept silent as he steered along the high street towards Fi's childhood home. Fi frowned as a movement near Effie's café caught her eye. She peered around, twisting to look over her shoulder as they passed.

She had just decided it was nothing and turned back to see a dark figure dart out in front of the car. Mort and Fi shrieked, and he hit the brakes, flinging both of them forward against their seatbelts. The figure stared in shock, caught in the headlights of the large car. Fi recognised the gothic customer from earlier in the day. The girl's eyes flashed in fear, and she ran off.

Fi struggled with her seatbelt and flung the car door open. "Wait!" She took a few stumbling steps over the tarmac, following in the direction the girl had headed. Cursing, she removed the stupid high-heeled shoes, intending to give chase.

Running footsteps sounded through the empty streets, echoing away from the road. Mort got out of the car and stared in the direction the girl had run, but she had disappeared.

"She's gone."

Fi stopped, one shoe in hand and shook her head. "I hope she's OK. What's she doing out alone at night?"

Mort shrugged and checked his watch. "It's not that late and who knows what teenagers get up to these days…"

"Do you know how old you sound?"

"Old enough not to have to worry about running for the bus. Speaking of… don't want to get dinged." He ducked back into the car and closed the door as the bus pulled out around the stationary vehicle. The driver beeped the horn and scowled as he passed.

Fi retreated to the pavement and watched the advert for the latest action movie pasted to the side of the country bus. Apparently, a superhero stuck in time was big blockbuster stuff. Once the bus had made it past, she headed back to the passenger side.

"Do you think that's all she was doing?"

"No idea, but I do know if I don't get you back on time, your mum might turn me into a frog."

"Nah, she's more likely to turn errant boyfriends into rats."

"Boyfriend?"

Fi looked away. "Just an expression."

She didn't miss Mort's grin as he pulled out and headed to the witch's house. The lights were on in the kitchen as the doctor steered his way to the parking at the rear of the house. He insisted on walking her to the door. Fi made it all the way to the step before she stumbled again in her uncomfortable shoes and fell against the doctor.

He caught her and held her tight against his warm body for a moment. She tensed in his arms initially before looking up into his dark eyes. The moon reflected in her own blue eyes, making them seem impossibly large. He bent his head to hers. Something edged into his legs, followed by a hacking sound. They broke apart and stared as Cressida hacked up something warm, wet and overall disgusting onto Mort's feet. His eyes widened with surprise and disgust as he shook his wet shoe.

Fi stammered an apology, a wave of shame and embarrassment flowing through her, mortified by her familiar's behaviour.

You're back, I see.

The voice was followed by sharp claws pricking her calves as Cressida stretched up, wanting comfort. Fi reached down absentmindedly to stroke the small lizard's head, pulling herself out of Mort's arms, not wondering how she knew the small wyrm wanted reassurance.

About time too. I'm starving.

"I'm not surprised, you've just thrown up on my date," Fi muttered before realising she sounded like she was talking to herself. "Er, Mort, this is Cressy, ouch! I mean Lady Cressida Charmington, my, um, familiar. Sorry, she gets testy when she's hungry."

Testy! I do not get testy.

"Hello Lady Cressida, what a fine wyrm you are." He bent down and scratched Cressida behind her scaly ears, discreetly ignoring the lump of smouldering wyrm puke on his smart suede shoes.

I like him. The small golden wyrm let out a purr of pleasure and wound herself around the doctor's legs, avoiding her own vomit.

"I think she likes you."

"Of course, she does, I'm charming."

"And so modest!"

"Well…"

The door opened, and the lights flickered on and off. Fi sighed. Between familiars and protective houses, it was likely that she would remain single forever.

"Sorry, I'd better go before the house turns on the sprinklers."

Mort laughed, then took in Fi's serious expression. "You're not joking?"

The tech witch squirmed. "It has happened before…"

"Oh, I want to hear that story!"

"Next time, maybe."

The lights dimmed again, and Fi smiled. In a daring burst, she stood on her tiptoes and kissed the tall doctor on his cheek before she disappeared inside, the golden wyrm at her heels.

Once inside, Fi kicked off her shoes and absentmindedly dished out a couple of scoops of charcoal for her familiar before heading to her room. The house lights turned themselves on as she walked upstairs, switching off once she had passed each swinging chandelier. She sank onto the bed and stared up at the ceiling. Her phone buzzed. A grin spread across her face, Mort was texting her already, so this was what it was like to be happy in a relationship. She checked the screen, careful to keep her feelings tightly under control so she didn't fry the circuits; she didn't need to fork out for another phone this year. Fi blinked as she read the message.

Saw this and thought of you.

A picture of a forked lightning bolt was attached to the message. It wasn't from Mort, as she'd expected, hoped even. The text was from Maximillian Baskerville, Maxi to his friends, and brought some swirling feelings with it. He was charming, in a bumbling sort of way. They'd worked together to save the people of Avalon and he'd been genuinely interested in her magic and what she could do, which was a first for Fi, but while engineering a tablet to communicate between worlds, she had fried him with her powers. Which sort of put a dampener on any budding relationship. And now he was texting her.

Fi lay awake for a long time as the date played through her mind, her confusing friendship with Maxi edging into her thoughts. Eventually, she fell into a fitful sleep, dreaming of texts, curries, choking, and the scared girl who had run out in front of a car.

Chapter 10

The next day brought a flurry of activity as Fi baked a batch of fluffy scones to take to Effie's shop. She had had an epiphany overnight. Not about her love life, which was now confusing as heck since Maxi had texted. No, she'd had a brainwave on how to sort Effie's stock system and was keen to put it in place. The scones were an added bonus to sweeten the ageing shop owner over, plus earn her a bit of extra cash and keep Nell off her case.

But first, there was breakfast to serve. Nell was in the garden, picking fruit from the thriving trees in the small orchard at the end of the garden. No matter the time of year, the trees were full of perfectly ripe fruit thanks to a combination of Nell's nature magic and whatever powered the witch's house.

Fi cooked up a full English while her scones baked. She absentmindedly fed a charred piece of vegan bacon to Cressida before plating up the rest for their guest. Cressida nosed the burned offering and then swiped it away with her front foot. Fi couldn't have agreed with the sentiment more.

It was strange, Fi thought, how people chose to avoid meat, but still wanted to taste it. She turned to the pan that had her own, pig original bacon sizzling in its own fat and flipped it up onto a thick piece of white bread for later.

Cressida eyed the fresh bacon, her nostrils widening and drool forming at the corner of her mouth.

"Don't even think about it," Fi warned, reaching for a pot of coffee and plonking it onto a tray. Her own mouth watered at the scent of bacon and she wiped away her saliva. She must be hungry, she didn't normally get so worked up about food...but, then it was bacon, sweet, delicious rashers of goodness.

I don't know what you're talking about.

"If my bacon is gone when I get back from delivering breakfast, you're sleeping outside."

It's odd. She doesn't smell like Ophelia.

"What?" Fi couldn't follow the subject change.

The lady staying here. She smells different.

"Why would she smell like Effie?" Fi screwed up her face, trying to understand the golden wyrm.

Cressida stretched out like a cat, then turned in a circle before settling down in the exact same spot she'd been sitting in before.

People in the same family smell alike.

"So, I smell like Agatha to you?"

Not exactly the same, the wyrm admitted. *You have a more charcoal, crackling smell than your sister and your mother. They both smell of the earth. And you should use the matching tea set for a guest.*

Fi ignored the creature's comment about the crockery and continued to bundle mismatched plates onto the tray. She filled up the ceramic toast rack with generous slices of homemade bread, then paused.

"So, what does Adriana smell like?"

Salt and death.

"Bit dramatic. And Effie?"

Ophelia has an air of lavender and old paper. It's quite pleasant.

"Well, they are quite distant relatives…great niece, that's three generations apart and it's not like they've lived together or even near each other. Maybe she comes from a coastal town. That would explain the salt."

Cressida flicked her tail in disagreement.

"What are you saying, then?"

I'm saying it's odd. That's all. You should watch them.

"I have things to do today. You watch them if you're so worried about it."

Maybe I will.

"Really, you could use the matching china Fiona, what will our guest think! Quick, switch out the side plate for the one with cats. There, now it matches. Go on then, take it in, the food's getting cold." Nell placed two fresh pears on the tray and shooed Fi in the direction of the dining room where guests breakfasted.

Fi kicked the adjoining door open and went through, Cressida at her heels. Their single paying guest occupied a table in the centre of the room, reading something from a small journal. Adriana was dressed in a fitted yellow designer dress that matched the shade of her stiletto heeled shoes exactly. Fi wondered how anyone could be that co-ordinated. Adriana put down the small leather-bound pocketbook she had been looking at and smiled up at her server.

"Morning, here's your breakfast." Fi placed the silver tray on the pressed white tablecloth and began to unload the plates, placing each item onto the surface carefully so she didn't spill anything. She stepped back, tray in hand. Cressida curled up on a cushioned chair in the corner of the room. Spying on people was hard work, but somebody had to do it.

"Thank you ever so much, that's very kind of you to make a vegan breakfast."

"No problem. Can I get you anything else?"

"No, thank you."

Fi turned to hurry back into the kitchen.

"Actually….there is one thing…"

"Yes?" Fi spun round and tried not to shift from foot to foot. Her scones only had about a minute left.

"I wonder, would you mind frightfully if I had a refresh on my coffee? I can't seem to drink enough in the mornings. With oat milk, naturally." Adriana gave a little laugh.

"Of course, anything else?"

"Is the marmalade organic? I only eat organic food."

"I'm sure it is, it's from the local farm."

"Lovely."

"Anything else?"

"No that will be all, unless…do you have any thin cut marmalade for the toast? I can't stand the thick cut."

"I'll have a look in the kitchen." Fi took a step towards the door.

"And I don't suppose there's any HP sauce to go with the bacon?"

"I'm sure we have some somewhere…" Fi waited expectantly. Adriana smiled politely at her. "Will that be all?"

"Yes, thank you." The young woman picked up her knife and fork and began to delicately slice her food.

Fi gathered up the requested marmalade and HP sauce and headed back to the dining room where Adriana talked some nonsense about the weather and her Mum asked for some help with the website.

"Mum! You have to keep up to date with the latest software. Here." She settled down to install the latest update and forgot all about the scones until Adriana sniffed the air.

"Is something burning?"

Fi barged back into the kitchen and raced to the oven. She opened the door and sighed with dismay as the smell of burned cake filled her nose. She had been too long, and the scones were ruined. She took them out and placed them on the marble side, biting her lip as she wondered if she could save them, maybe cut off the blackened tops. Behind her, the smoke alarm began to beep.

With a sigh, she turned to her sandwich, and swore as she saw the greasy imprints where two perfect rashers of bacon had sat.

"Cressida!"

Chapter 11

There was no bacon left in the fridge and Fi tried not to think about how pathetic she was as she savoured the greasy remnants of her sandwich. She worked out her annoyance on a new set of dough and got a successful batch of golden scones out of the oven before setting off to the café.

"Oh, hello love, what can I do for you?"

"Er, I'm here with the scones you asked for, and I've had a thought about your inventory…" Fi cut herself off.

"Yes, yes, that sounds lovely. You do whatever you think is best." Effie patted the tech witch on her arm absentmindedly. "I'll be in the reading room if you need me."

Fi watched her go with a frown and peeked into the cat diary next to the counter. No appointments for today. She shook her head and started unloading the scones onto one of the display stands before covering them with the see-through plastic case that protected the baked goods from flies. There were a couple of large moist cakes already on the counter. She moved the stands around, gauging the best positions until she was satisfied. She appraised the display. Not bad. A little rustic perhaps, but that added to the charm.

Having done that, she wiped down the coffee machine and prepared for customers. Effie's premonition of a coachload of tourists proved to be accurate and by half past ten the small shop was packed, and Fi was run ragged making coffees, teas and cutting slices of Victoria sponge cake as customers took pictures of the quaint interior.

As the witch relaxed after the tourists finally had their fill and left to walk around Omensford's cobbled streets, Effie appeared.

"Oh, you're still here?"

"Er, yes, it's been pretty busy. Are you alright?"

"Yes, fine. I've been communing with the spirits. I haven't been able to get a straight answer, but knowing her, I can bet why she's here."

"Er...knowing who?"

"I don't know how much time I'll have. Best to get rid of it. Yes, yes, that's the best thing." Fi got the impression that Effie wasn't talking to her. Suddenly, the old witch's eyes fixed on Fi with a strange glint. "I can trust you, can't I, Fiona?"

"Of course you can, but..."

"Take this." She thrust a small velvet bag into Fi's hands.

"What is it?"

"Don't open it here! She might be able to sense it. I've *seen* that you are the only one who can protect it, maybe the magic of the house can help you. You have to keep it from her. If it gets into her hands…"

"Who's hands?"

"Adriana's!"

"What are you talking about?"

Effie took a deep breath. "In that bag is a relic of times long past. It will show you your deepest desire…and if she had it…" Effie shuddered.

"I don't understand."

"It's…" Effie looked over her shoulder at the door. "Hide it!"

Fi panicked at the old lady's screech and shoved the bag into the pocket of her hoody just before the shop bell announced another customer. Adriana strode in, her stiletto shoes clacking on the floor. She removed her oversized sunglasses and looked around the shop.

"What a lovely…place. So…quaint." On her lips, the compliment sounded like an insult.

"Thank you, dear, and look at you, all dressed up to see little old me. Such a clever idea too, glasses that cover up your entire face."

Adriana's smile froze as she tried to work out if she'd been insulted.

"As you don't seem busy, I thought it would be good to have our little chat."

"Of course, no time like the present."

Fi shuffled from foot to foot, uncomfortable at the family reunion she didn't understand. Her own family might not be perfect, but at least they were open with each other. Adriana stared pointedly at her.

"Why don't you take the afternoon off, love, here's something for your trouble. Now go home." Effie laced the last word with meaning and stuffed a wad of notes from the till into Fi's hand before eyeing the perfectly dressed witch standing by the counter. "Me and my great-niece need to have a little talk."

Chapter 12

Fi's feet led her to the corner shop where she used her newfound wealth, which on closer inspection was about forty quid, to buy a deluxe chocolate coated ice cream. She glanced at the newspaper stand as she joined the queue, noting the blurred shot of a familiar half dwarf who had saved her life in Avalon. Amethyst was mid stride next to her tall elven prince as they crossed a street in Cardiff. Above the picture was a headline about Lorandir being 'elf't holding a baby'. Fi groaned. The headline writer had probably high-fived the team when they'd come up with that one.

She got to the front of the queue and paid Mr Kumar for the magnum. Outside, she stripped off her hoody and tied it round her waist in the warmth of the late spring day, the odd shaped package Effie had given her making a strange weight by her thighs. Unwrapping her ice cream, she headed to the park to eat her unexpected treat.

At this time of day, it was full of small kids with their parents ignoring them from the side-lines, but within shouting distance if a young child got stuck in the climbing frame. A group of teenagers skulked around the half pipe that the local council had built in one of their attempts to appeal to the hip youth of today and encourage them to skateboard instead of vandalising the town. The weather was too sunny, though, and the cries of children too raucous for the gang of cool kids, and they soon slumped off.

Fi sat on a worn bench in the shade next to a dad scrolling through social media as his offspring yelled various versions of "Watch me! Look what I can do, Dad!" from every single piece of playground equipment.

Fi got out her own phone and checked her messages. There was one from the recruiting site she'd registered with suggesting jobs she might be suitable for. It seemed like they'd emailed her anything that had the word 'technology' in the title, including an advert for a cleaner for a local IT firm. She sighed, trying to decide if it was worth sorting through or whether she should look for jobs directly.

Another email caught her attention. An interview! She scanned the message to make sure it wasn't junk before reading it more closely. Yes, she had applied for the distributed role at the global IT firm. She quickly fired back a response that she was available for an interview next week and in her excitement, did a fist pump in the park. She looked round, embarrassed at displaying her joy so publically, but no one was paying her any attention.

"Dad! Dad!"

Fi smiled; she couldn't help it. This could be her chance to get her life back on track, to move back into her own place and, more importantly, to get out of her mother's house. She checked the salary information again and her grin grew broader. She finished up her ice cream and tore her gaze away from her phone to find a bin.

"Dad! Dad!"

Fi searched for the source of the panicked voice. A small child dangled from the monkey bars, unable to swing to the next one and their grip was starting to slip. Fi surveyed the park. Only one man wasn't looking up. She elbowed the man sitting next to her. He stared at her, annoyed at the interruption to his word game.

"Is that your son?" Fi pointed to the small boy now screaming in distress as his sweaty fingers slipped further.

The man leapt up and raced across the recycled tyre flooring to catch his son. He got there just as the boy's grip failed and they tumbled to the ground in a heap. They got up a couple of seconds later, the dad hugging the small child and promising ice creams as long as he didn't tell mum.

Fi went back to scrolling on her screen. A shadow fell over her. She looked up, squinting, and smiled at the familiar face.

"Hi Steve, what are you doing here?"

"Just taking Zadie to the park. She needs to burn off some energy."

Fi looked at Zadie. Steve and Glen's adopted daughter was picking up every stone she could find within the metal railings that marked out the playground as separate from the football field.

"What's she doing?"

"Looking for fairies. It's her new obsession. How're things?"

"Good, actually, I've got a job interview."

"That's great news! What's the role?"

"Tech consulting."

"Right, you've always loved computers, haven't you? I wish I could do something like that."

"What, work with computers?" Fi frowned. For all Steve's skills, she hadn't thought he was good with IT.

"No, can you imagine?!" Steve paused as a fire engine zoomed past, sirens blaring. "I mean do something I love, like baking. I wish I could have a full-time job doing that."

"Right, yeah." Fi squirmed a little. She did love computers. But there was a world of difference between playing online games or solving the problems of upgrading her personal computer and asking people if they had turned it on and off again.

Fi was saved from further conversation by Zadie running over. "Fairies don't like it when you pull their wings off, so you shouldn't do it," the girl said, completely deadpan.

"That's right dear."

Fi tried not to stare. Another fire engine roared past the park. "What do you think the matter is?"

Steve looked round and sniffed the air. "Not sure, but there's smoke coming from the high street."

Fi stood and walked to the road, leaving Steve and his creepy daughter to play. She was at the end of the main road when she saw the smoke billowing out of Effie's café.

Chapter 13

Fi skidded to a halt just outside the police cordon that had already been set up and panted after her sudden exertion to get to the shop.

She took in the scene. Firefighters fought to get the blaze under control and prevent the fire spreading to the neighbouring shops. A small crowd had gathered. Sita weaved through the crowd taking action shots for the local paper. Fi's fingers itched. Not for the first time, she wished she had more useful magic. Electricity couldn't help to fight the roaring flames.

She recognised Detective Ledd and nodded hello. He caught her eye and gave her a curt nod back. She had been under suspicion of poisoning late last year, and he was still annoyed that he couldn't work out how the real culprit had vanished. Given Fi had been involved in her disappearance, he still considered her to be a suspicious person.

He went back to talking to Adriana, who was seated in the back of an ambulance, huddled up in a blanket. Somehow, she looked smaller than she had done earlier.

Fi edged around to get closer to the ambulance and ducked under the cordon. She got right up to the detective's side before he noticed her.

"What do you think you're doing? Civilians stay behind the tape. It's dangerous to be back here!"

"Yes, detective, only I know Adriana, well she's staying with us, so I thought…"

"Oh, let her stay with me, dear. It's nice to see a familiar face." Adriana surprised Fi by speaking up.

"Alright, if it's what you want." The detective sounded dubious, and Fi didn't press it. "Is there anything else you can tell me?"

The young woman slumped forward. "It's all gone, a life's work ruined."

"Where's Effie?"

Adriana looked up, startled. "I didn't see her leave."

Fi frowned. "Then she's still in there!" She ran towards the fire fighters. "Oi, there's someone in there! Someone's trapped inside!"

A ripple of noise went around the bystanders. The firemen and women redoubled their efforts to dampen the blaze enough so that they could enter. A hand landed on Fi's shoulder.

"That's enough now. Let them do their job."

She turned to look into Detective Ledd's podgy face. His expression was part annoyance, part compassion. She shrugged him off and trouped back to the ambulance. Adriana watched the fire with tears in her eyes.

"I'll miss the old girl."

"You got along then, in the end?" Fi asked, blinking away her own tears. Effie had been a constant in her life for, well, for all of it.

"I wouldn't say that exactly, but she will be missed."

Fi thought that was odd phrasing, but maybe Effie's great niece was in shock.

"Do you have anyone you want to call?" Fi stuck to practical things she could do.

Adriana gave that some thought before shaking her head. "She was the only family I had."

"We don't know she's dead yet."

The young woman shot Fi a look of sympathy but stayed silent.

"Can I get you anything?" Fi turned her thoughts away from the fire.

"No thanks, I've got sweet tea." Adriana lifted her mug to confirm that she did indeed have a cup of tea. "That's the thing that gets you through life's troubles, isn't it? A nice cup of tea. Do you want one, love?"

Fi made a grunt of assent and stared at the shop, waiting for some sign that Effie was alive. She was a powerful witch with premonition for goodness' sake, she couldn't just die in a fire. It took an age, then there was a rush of activity as two firemen managed to get into the building.

"Do you want to call your mum?" Adriana interrupted her concentration.

Fi took out her phone and stared at it. What was she even meant to say? She called her sister first. Agatha was always better at emotional stuff.

"What's going on? I saw you sprinting out of the park!"

"You were there?"

"I just arrived; you ran straight past us."

"OK, there's been a fire."

"What? Are you OK? Is Mum OK? Oh goddess, Bea get your things now, we're leaving."

"No, no, we're fine. It was at the café."

There was a long pause.

"Good, well good that you're alright. Is Effie...?"

At that moment, a fireman stepped out of the building cradling something. He walked towards a waiting stretcher and two paramedics.

"No, oh no, no, no!" Fi ran forward, forgetting about her sister on the line.

The detective and one of the fire fighters restrained her as she fought to get a closer look. A paramedic pulled a white sheet up over the tiny figure.

"I'm so sorry," Detective Ledd said.

Fi slumped and stopped fighting to get closer. The voice coming out of her phone finally registered with her brain.

"Fi! What is going on? Answer me! Fi!"

"Oh Aggy…Effie's dead."

Chapter 14

Witches' funerals happened quickly after a death was confirmed. They didn't like the bodies to hang around in case uninformed people got ideas about taking pieces to try and get the power that a magic user wielded. That might sound like a strange belief, but given the grave looting that had gone on less than a hundred years before, it was one that witches stood by. Ophelia Harrington's funeral was no exception.

Once the death certificate had been formally signed by the on-call doctor, Effie's body was released to her next of kin. Adriana was in a daze following the fire and gladly handed over the organisation to Nell Blair.

Nell immediately arranged for special permission to cremate the body in the traditional way; by fire. So it was that Effie's body lay in a wicker coffin, hastily constructed by the nature witches in the coven and two days later, the WWWI gathered at the local crematorium.

On the outside, the brick building was much like any other crematorium. A sombre and reassuring place where people knew that their dead relative was in expert hands, used to dealing with death and its trappings.

Inside, the main hall was a bright white with no decorations on the wall other than the brightly coloured stained-glass windows that allowed sunlight to paint the room. Unlike other crematoria, however, the Cotswolds Crematorium was run by a wizard with an affinity for fire. Rupert Tine was a timid man who had inherited the family business from his father, who had inherited it from his father and so on down the line of Tines to the present day.

He stepped up to the small lectern at the front of the room and looked out over the small number of assembled witches, wizards, and warlocks. There would be a memorial service at a later date so more people could pay their respects, but today only the immediate Omensford coven was present,

"Ophelia Harrington, known to her friends as 'Effie', was ahead of her time. She was a colourful figure in the Cotswolds and always ready to help anybody in need. She ran a local business, which was well-loved by villagers and tourists alike. I know her generous portions of cake and the eclectic mix of items she sold will carry on in many people's memories. Effie enjoyed taking part in the community and frequently donated her leftover baked goods to a local homeless charity.

"Effie was a loyal friend, and she was particularly loyal to the Witches', Wizards' and Warlocks' Institute, where she served as Secretary of the Omensford branch for the past fifty-three years. She loved attending their social events, and I know she will be sorry to miss the upcoming Spring Social.

"She leaves behind a gaping hole in our small community and, more particularly, she leaves behind a newly reunited family. I will now handover to Adriana Harrington, her great niece and Eleanor Blair, her good friend to say a few words."

Adriana stepped forward, stumbling a little on her high-heeled shoes. She coughed once as she placed a small piece of paper on the lectern and read, "I feel like I have known Effie for a long time, and I know she would be so touched to see you all here today. She loves, loved, Omensford and cared for everyone here. She dedicated her life to the village and in a way, it's fitting that her shop has burned out along with her body. I thought a lot about what I wanted to say and it's simply this: thank you. Thank you all for coming and thank you for the joy you brought into her life."

The young woman ended with a flourish that was so like Effie, it made Fi smile, before she hurried back to her pew, wobbling in her high heels and wiping away a tear.

Fi's mother, Nell Blair, held her head high as she stepped up to take Adriana's place. "I knew Effie well and I can remember when we first met, at a Spring Social back in…well far be it for me to reveal a lady's age, suffice to say it was a number of years ago. She spotted me standing on my own and forced me to dance with the man who would later become my husband. I still sometimes wonder if she knew what she did that day, but of course she did. It was one of her gifts.

"Effie supported me, as she did with many of us, throughout our lives; both the glad times and the unhappy times. She was blessed with a prescience more powerful than any witch I know and, though she struggled with her knowledge of the future, she never let it overwhelm her. She was a good friend to me, and a great support when we worked together in the WWWI later in my life. It is in her honour that, this year, we will dedicate the Spring Social to our dear friend Ophelia."

Adriana burst into tears at Nell's declaration, along with many other members of the congregation.

Rupert stepped back to the front of the room. "Now, it is clear from speaking to many of you here today that Effie knew her own mind, and she was never one to do things by the book as it were. So, by special request, I will commit Ophelia Harrington's body to flames in the form she wished."

The fire wizard stepped towards the wicker coffin and pressed the button that moved the conveyor belt into the unlit furnace. He waited until Effie's body was fully inside before he closed his eyes and motioned with his hands.

A flaming phoenix erupted from his fingers. The fire bird flew in a circuit of the room, drawing everyone's eyes. The flames grew from deep red to bright yellow to white. Beads of sweat on Rupert's forehead glinted in the firelight as he poured his power into the creation. The flaming phoenix beat its wings and flew higher and higher to the rafters of the open hall before it dived, speeding into the opening of the large furnace. The coffin disappeared into an inferno before Rupert pressed the button to close the doors. And so Effie's body was cremated.

The gathered magic users let out a sigh of relief. Now their friend could be assured peace, and no one could steal her bones for their magic or try to reanimate the powerful witch with necromancy. They waited respectfully as the body burned. Confronted with mortality, many of the congregation mused on their own memories of Effie. They shuffled in their seats as the minutes mounted.

Adriana stood. "There's tea and refreshments at the back for those who want them."

The witches and wizards gratefully made their way to the back of the hall where a folding table laden with biscuits and a steaming metal urn full of tea waited for them. Rupert's wife, used to dealing with mourners, respectfully poured the refreshments and didn't ask any stupid questions about the weather or how anyone's day was going.

Nell patted Adriana's arm. "That was well done."

The young woman smiled in acknowledgement of the compliment and then hurried off to join the growing queue. Somehow, she made it to the front and was soon nursing a plain white mug of sweet, milky tea while eating a chocolate covered digestive biscuit.

"It must run in the family, that's exactly what Effie would have done," Agatha said, wiping away a tear.

Nell smiled at the memory of her friend. "She was always the first one in the queue for hot drinks and biscuits. No matter the occasion." She looked around the room. "I hope I'm remembered this warmly when I'm gone."

Her daughters exchanged glances before hugging their mother. A tear crept down Nell's cheek. It was the first time either Fi or Agatha had seen her cry.

Nell patted each of them on the back before sniffing and pulling away. Agatha disappeared to get her a hot drink while Fi tried to think what she could say that could help her mother.

"Er, I've got a job interview coming up."

Nell blinked at her in shock and Fi could see her mother readjusting her emotions to deal with this revelation. "That's good news. And do you think you're ready to work?"

"Mum! You've been badgering me to stop feeling sorry for myself and find something to do with my life!"

"That's *my* job. I'm your mother. What is the role?"

"Tech consultant."

"Oh."

"I thought you'd be more excited than that. It might mean I can move back out."

"Well, I'm glad you're looking and of course I want you to find a job, but you must know that I also want you to be happy so don't feel you have to take the first thing that comes along."

"OK...but I like working in tech."

"Alright then, you know best, I'm sure."

Fi narrowed her eyes. That wasn't something her mother would normally say. She tried to work out her mum's angle. "What does that mean?"

"What are you talking about? I want to support my youngest daughter and suddenly I'm subject to the Spanish Inquisition!"

"OK, OK." Fi held her hands up placatingly. Somewhere in the conversation, she was now at fault. Fi took a cup from Agatha, who had hovered at the end of the pew during the exchange.

Adriana appeared, wiping crumbs of chocolate biscuit from her plump lips. "Everything alright?"

Agatha took a slurp from her own drink, without spilling a drop while handing the other mug to Nell. "I'm not exactly sure but I think Fi might have a new job." She beamed at her sister.

"Exciting news. You've been at home for a while now, haven't you? Are you going to be alright on your own, Nell, if Fi moves back out?"

"I'm sure Mum will be fine." Fi frowned. "You've lived alone before. I always thought you rather enjoyed it, none of your daughters getting under your feet."

Nell kept silent and sipped her tea. Before Fi could think too hard about her mother feeling lonely if she moved out, Rupert Tine approached, cradling something between his arms.

Rupert coughed. "I have the ashes here." He held out the traditionally shaped urn. It was fashioned from purple stone, accented by a golden band that ran around the neck and matched the gold lid that sat securely on top.

Both Nell and Adriana reached out to take the ashes. There was a pause. Followed by an uncomfortable smile. Then a polite cough.

"It's tradition for the next of kin to take the ashes," Rupert tried.

Nell stared at him for a long moment before she lowered her arms.

Fi and Agatha let out the breaths they had been holding and shared a look. Adriana cradled the urn carefully in her arms before walking outside.

Chapter 15

Fi found Adriana sitting on a bench. She hadn't wanted to find anyone. The tech witch had wanted some space away from her mother and had disappeared out of the building for a walk before she could restart any conversations about her job opportunity.

She had expected Nell to be ecstatic that she was getting back onto the job market and thinking about moving out again, but her mother had surprised her. Now she was questioning whether she was ready. After all, only a few months ago, her power had been so out of control, someone had died. And did it matter that they were a murderer?

What's to say she wouldn't hurt someone close next time? Again. Fi shook her head as the childhood memory of her mother looking up at her in fear flooded her mind. She was too volatile, too dangerous. And she didn't want to hurt family or friends again.

It was in the middle of those thoughts that she found the younger woman seated on a bench, one hand resting on the golden lid of the urn while she stared into the middle distance. The other hand absent-mindedly rubbed her foot, which she had eased out of the pointed shoes. Fi turned to walk away. Her converse trainers scrunched loudly on the gravel path, startling the woman from her thoughts.

"Hello."

"Hello." Fi looked at a large tree growing nearby, then the ground, then at the other woman in her neat black dress. "Did you want some company?"

She fervently hoped the answer would be 'No'. She wasn't good with people at the best of times and the cremation of a family member didn't exactly count as a good time.

Adriana patted the bench next to her and Fi took a seat reluctantly. Unsure what to say to a grieving great niece, Fi kept quiet and scuffed her shoes on the ground.

"I never thought I'd have to deal with the after part of my funeral…and now I'm here, I have no idea."

Fi frowned, trying to follow the grieving woman's words.

"I mean, what would you like done with your ashes?"

Fi nodded as she finally understood Adriana's dilemma. She shrugged. "I'm not sure it would help you, but I think it would be cool to be made into a computer." Adriana frowned and Fi elaborated, "They can make ashes into diamonds under pressure, right? So, people are experimenting with using diamonds to replace silicon chips and…" Fi noticed Adriana's eyes glaze over. "…I thought that would be kind of cool. A way to keep on living after I've died."

104

The younger witch nodded at that. "To keep on living after the body has died. Yes, that's the dream, isn't it? But what to do with these?"

"Some people like to have their ashes scattered somewhere that meant something to them. Or I read online about one company that can turn your ashes into a firework."

Adriana shook her head. "It's amazing what they can do nowadays. How much things have moved on since I was young."

"Come on, you can't be older than thirty," Fi scoffed. "Sorry, that was insensitive."

Adriana's hand went to her face, smoothing her soft, unlined cheek. "Not to worry. I'm older than I look and...I was just...thinking too much."

Both women sat in contemplative silence for a few minutes. The sharp sound of feet on gravel made them both turn towards the crematorium.

Mort approached apologetically. "Nell said to tell you that they're going home, if you'd like a lift," he spoke quietly to Adriana.

"Thank you, I think I'll call a taxi. I want to think about things on my own."

"I'm so sorry for your loss."

Adriana smiled sadly, and when she spoke, her voice was somehow sharper than it had been before. "It's such a shame that she went like that, but in a way, perhaps it's what she would have wanted."

105

"What do you mean?" Fi asked.

"The inquest finished and a detective called me with the results. The fire was started by a beam of sunlight magnified through one of Effie's crystal balls."

Fi jumped to her feet. "That's what they think happened? You're sure?"

Fi ran, the gravel scrunching under her feet.

"Wait! Where are you going?" Adriana called after her.

"There's no way Effie left a crystal ball uncovered. She was killed."

Chapter 16

Fi fumed in her room. The house creaked as she paced up and down over the carpet. No one had listened to her. Adriana had tried to talk her out of saying anything. Mort had actually suggested she 'calm down'. And her mother had just looked at her blankly, trying to compute what her daughter was saying.

She had called the police anyway. Obviously. Detective Ledd had been less than considerate when she'd explained her theory. She could still remember his scathing tone.

"Let me get this straight, Ms Blair. You have no evidence at all. Just a thought that she wouldn't have left a crystal ball uncovered. And you want me to open a murder investigation based on your hunch?"

"Ummm..."

The detective's voice took on an understanding tone, which was somehow worse than his outright disbelief. "I don't mean to be unkind, but Ms Harrington was in her nineties. I mean, *I* forget why I go into a room nowadays…so it's not surprising that she'd forget to put a crystal ball away. Anyway, what I'm saying is that the forensic fire investigator was quite clear on the cause. I understand you were close to Ms Harrington, but it's best not to go round upsetting people with wild theories and move on."

He hung up on her. Fi glared at the phone as if it was personally to blame for the detective's words.

Maybe you should let dead witches lie…

Fi narrowed her eyes at her familiar as her fingers tapped to their own rhythm against her thighs.

"Was that what you thought when your first witch died?"

A wisp of smoke curled from the wyrm's right nostril and her eyes narrowed. *Goody Winships was murdered–*

"So was Effie." Fi felt her emotions boil and her power threatened to surface as she stared down her familiar.

Cressida returned Fi's glare. *If you're so sure, why are you wearing a hole in the carpet here?*

She was too worked up to consider why her anger flared so hard, when she could normally tolerate her familiar's needling, but then the hot flash of anger that had filled Fi's chest dimmed. Fi stopped pacing and sat down forcefully in her ergonomic computer chair. She would do something. She started up the PC, intending to log on to an online game and blow something up to work out some of her frustration, but as she moved the mouse, she paused on a different application.

In a sort of trance, Fi opened up the notice board programme she had created to help her get through her studies. It helped her to think and organise her thoughts away from the constraints of pen and paper. And she'd most recently used it to solve the murder of a local WWWI Chairwoman.

With a few clicks, she opened up a new board and started filling out what she knew. It wasn't much. All she had were Sita's pictures, now on the local paper's website. They were capitalising on the most exciting news in six months by running a week's worth of articles about Effie and fire. Today's was an obituary in honour of Effie's funeral, but yesterday's had been about fire prevention. The article was punctuated with pictures of the burning shop under the headline; *All your burning questions about fire safety answered.*

Fi studied the photos carefully and saved them onto her virtual notice board. There were more pictures of the aftermath from the day of the fire. Fi clicked through shots of Adriana sitting in the back of an ambulance. Not one of them showed her in focus. Fi scrolled on. A figure in the crowd caught her eye. Fi zoomed in. Was it her imagination or did the teenager she'd served a few short days ago look guilty? Fi quickly made the goth girl suspect number one.

She searched for Effie online and, other than the obituary and some mentions of her shop in the local paper, found nothing.

After a few moments' thought, she searched for Effie's great niece. Nothing. Odd. Most people had some sort of social media presence. Fi tried to find a clear picture of the young woman to do an image match, but there was nothing from the day of the fire. Sita's photographic skills were slipping. Fi slapped a large question mark over Adriana.

She went back to the articles as if she might discover something new by rereading them and a comment stopped her. Gracey72 had written that Effie was an old fraud who tricked people out of their hard-earned money with fake psychic readings.

Fi frowned. Effie had given a reading to someone not too long before she was killed, and they hadn't been happy with the answers they'd got. Fi tried to remember more about the conversation, there was something about money; that could be a motive.

A quick search soon brought up Gracey72's email address and from there, Fi found social media handles and a physical address. The online complainant was number two on her suspect list.

She rushed out of her bedroom, struggling to get a jacket on over her Pokémon t-shirt. Now she had a purpose. Find Gracey72 and the goth girl. She almost bumped into Adriana, who had just unlocked her own bedroom door.

Fi peered into the room automatically, always interested in how the house had chosen to decorate for guests. Adriana's room was more cluttered than Fi remembered it. Framed enlarged tarot cards in an art déco style hung on the wall and

Fi was sure she glimpsed a crystal ball next to the urn on the bedside table. She frowned. Those hadn't been there when Adriana had checked in.

Cressida sniffed around the threshold then turned her attention to the young woman's feet. Confusion roared through Fi's mind. What was going on? She didn't feel in control of her emotions any more.

Something's not right...

Adriana pulled the door shut. "Oh hello, love, are you off out?"

Fi nodded. She didn't want to say she was going to find a potential murderer, and that the longer she thought about it, she wasn't so sure the teenager was a viable suspect. But she might know something.

"It must be hard, moving back in with Nell after all those years living on your own..." Fi stayed silent. It was only later that she thought it was odd that Adriana knew anything about her life away from the B&B. "I'm going to get some dinner; do you want to join me?"

Fi paused, about to shake her head. Then she remembered the question mark she had placed over Adriana's picture.

"That sounds nice."

Are you crazy? There's something wrong about her. I can't quite place it but...

"Where did you have in mind?"

Oh, fine, just ignore me then. Don't worry, when they find your body, I'll be sure to tell your ghost that I told you so.

"How about Sorella's?" Adriana named the local Italian restaurant. "I just love their grilled steak – Tuscan style with that lemon and garlic." Her eyes turned misty, presumably at the thought of the tender piece of meat.

"Are you alright to walk or shall I get us a cab?" Fi looked pointedly at the younger woman's feet. She was sporting lower heels than at the cremation, but they still looked dangerously high to the tech witch.

Adriana followed her gaze. "Taxi, please. First thing tomorrow, I'm getting some new shoes, you've got to look after your feet, or they'll give you trouble once you hit seventy."

Be careful, will you? And tell your mother where you're going. And be back by ten, or I'll raise the alarm.

Fi gave a small 'hmm' of agreement, thinking what an odd turn of phrase Adriana had used for a woman who couldn't have been older than thirty, and dialled the local taxi firm.

She bent down and tickled Cressida behind her ear. Both her own and the wyrm's concern eased as the wyrm nuzzled her hand. "I'll be back soon, don't worry."

The two women walked to the road in silence and got into the cab. Sometimes she wished she'd learned how to drive, but it wasn't exactly like she travelled to a lot of places. Fi texted her mum to let her know she was going out. Nell replied telling her to be careful. Not for the first time, Fi wondered if her mother could read minds, because she was channelling Cressida's nervous energy to a tee.

112

Fi wondered if she should be worried about her mother. Nell had disappeared into the library as soon as they had returned from her friend's cremation and hadn't emerged. There really ought to be a manual for dealing with the death of a loved one, Fi mused.

The taxi ride was quiet. The women sat on opposite sides of the back seat and stared out of the window at the watery excuse for a sunset. Fi snuck glances at Adriana, but the other woman kept her gaze fixed on the countryside. It was a relief to get out of the cramped car and into the restaurant with its familiar cosy, brick décor and dome-shaped pizza oven. The warming smell of home-made Italian cooking made Fi's mouth water and almost dispelled the awkward silence. Almost.

They sipped the complimentary water that a server brought to their table without saying a word as the two women perused their menus. Fi regretted coming. This was turning into a painful social interaction and what exactly was she going to ask Adriana? Just blurt out over the starters that it was suspicious that she turned up about twenty-four hours before Effie was burned to a crisp and Fi couldn't find anything about her on the internet. It wasn't exactly great detective work.

Fi sipped her diet cola and tried to think. How would a normal person start a conversation with a stranger who might be a murderer?

"So, how are you finding Omensford?"

Adriana arched a perfectly shaped eyebrow. "Well, the village is lovely, but I can't say the last few days have been the best of my life."

"No, of course. Right."

The waiter interrupted to take their orders. Fi went for a pizza while Adriana chose a vegetable risotto.

"I thought you liked steak."

"Don't be silly, I'm vegan."

"Right." Something odd was going on, but Fi didn't know what. She scrabbled for something else to say. "Er, what do you do for a living?"

"I run a charitable foundation, donating money to archaeological excavations across the globe. But I don't think you're interested in the difficult weather conditions the team is facing in the Caribbean." Adriana's bright eyes speared the tech witch with their intensity. "We both know you have something you want to ask me. So, ask it."

Fi stirred her drink nervously with a straw, taken aback by the young woman's confrontation. She seemed so much older than she looked. "Er, I mean it's pretty suspicious, don't you think? You were in the shop when the fire started, but you got out and Effie...didn't."

"You think I killed her." It was a statement with a hint of a sneer in it.

"I don't know what I think, but I liked Effie, and I don't think she would have left a crystal ball uncovered when it wasn't in use. And I don't think she would have stayed in a burning building." There, she'd said it.

114

Adriana thought for a moment, then nodded. "You're right, she wouldn't have done either of those things. But if you're asking what happened, of course, I'll tell you."

Chapter 17

They were silent while a waiter in a black shirt brought their food to the table. Adriana tasted her risotto and smiled slightly before asking for more pepper but refusing the parmesan cheese. Fi toyed with cutting her pepperoni pizza before picking up a slice and taking a bite. She kept her eyes on the elegant younger woman as she ate.

Adriana took another elegant forkful before starting to talk. "Ophelia and I spoke. Then I left."

"You left?"

Adriana nodded and wiped her mouth daintily with a linen napkin. "I left. It was clear she wasn't exactly pleased to see me, and after I'd spent so long trying to find her." She sighed. "Anyway, I knew I wasn't wanted, so I went out to clear my head. I walked back past the shop and saw flames. I thought I saw Ophelia inside, so I went back in."

"You went back in?"

"Are you going to repeat everything I say? Yes. I went back in to try to rescue my great aunt. But the fire caught quickly and there was nothing I could do. I ran back outside, and I feel so guilty. I'll never get to talk to her again, and we'll never have a chance to patch things up." Adriana's voice choked on her words, and Fi had the awful thought that it was exactly how an actor would behave. She took another bite of her pizza, chiding herself for her uncharitable thoughts, it wasn't like she was an expert in human emotions.

"What did you have to patch up?"

Adriana took a sip of her mineral water. "I believe that Ophelia and her sister, my...grandmother, had a falling out. That's why she wasn't thrilled to see me."

"Do you know what it was about?"

"Ophelia stole something from her sister, but that's all I know."

Fi munched on her pizza as she thought. "Any idea what it was?"

"Some sort of family heirloom, but whatever it was is gone now."

Something nudged the back of Fi's mind, but it disappeared as she tried to concentrate on it.

"Is your pizza good?"

"Yes thanks, lovely," Fi replied automatically. "So, you believe it was an accident?"

"What else could it have been? The woman was getting on a bit, she was distracted and I'm sorry if our conversation had a part in that, but the fire started through the crystal ball."

"There wasn't anything else you noticed," a note of desperation crept into Fi's voice, "anything at all."

"I've told the police everything, except…" Adriana's eyes widened. "There was a noise from the back of the shop before I left. I'd completely forgotten. Ophelia thought it was mice, but you don't think…I mean it could have been someone waiting for me to go. Poor Aunt Ophelia."

"You think there was someone else in the shop?"

"Maybe. I should tell the police, though. Just in case. I'll call that detective straight away." She got up from the table and walked outside to make the call.

Fi chewed distractedly as she thought. So, Adriana hadn't even been in the café when the fire had started, but someone else had been.

Chapter 18

The next morning, Fi woke late and as puzzled as ever. The mysterious figure that Adriana had mentioned had played through her mind all night, seeping its way into her dreams. She still had no idea how to find the goth girl, but, she had another lead.

Fi got dressed with more care than usual and pulled on black leggings and a black slouchy dress over the top.

Going somewhere nice?

"I thought I'd find Gracey72. She's local."

Cressida nodded approvingly. *Good idea.*

"You think so?" Fi was suspicious. The wyrm was usually snide and slightly superior.

Of course. I'll come too.

Fi decided not to press it. If Cressida was being supportive, that was a good thing. It would be nice to have some company. Fi stopped in her tracks. She had never been someone who needed company before, was the familiar bond changing her? The witch squinted sideways at Cressida.

What is it?

"Nothing."

Then stop looking at me like that.

"Sorry."

Fi looked up the bus times to Magewell on her phone as they went downstairs and swore. The next one was in fifteen minutes. Fi grabbed a cup of coffee to go and a cereal bar from her mother's store, scooped up the wyrm and ran to the bus stop.

Fi arrived just as the driver closed the doors. She banged on the glass, and he opened them again with a grin. Fi mumbled her thanks, paid the fare and found a seat. It took a while to get to Magewell and Fi spent the time listening to a true crime podcast while staring out of the grimy window as the countryside rolled past. Cressida curled up on her lap and closed her eyes, small snorts blowing from her mouth as she slept.

They arrived in the town an hour later and half the bus exited alongside Fi, the rest staying on for the longer haul to Cirencester. Fi checked her phone again. According to Grace's social media page, she went to dog yoga about this time, so Fi made her way to the town hall, above the local library. Outside the door, she paused.

"Maybe this isn't such a good idea..."

You're here now.

"But…yoga…"

It won't kill you.

A pair of middle-aged ladies pushed past her and made their way upstairs in their figure-hugging lycra leggings, two rat-like dogs hopping up behind them. Fi huffed and followed them inside. She tramped up the stairs and huddled at the back, scanning the class for anyone who might be Gracey72. Fi frowned as she saw a familiar face and hurried over to take the spot next to Effie's client from the other week.

"Is this spot taken?"

"No, go ahead."

"I'm Fi."

"Grace. Nice to meet you."

"Have you been coming here long?"

"Almost a year now, Poppy here loves it, don't you?" Grace paused to stroke an excitable Labrador next to her. "And you? I haven't seen you here before."

"No, it's my first class." Fi was truthful.

"And where's your dog?" Grace looked around.

"Er…here. Her name's Cressida. She's a wyrm, but she thinks she's a dog."

Excuse me?

"Oh. Nice to meet you Cressida, such an unusual…name. Where's your mat?"

"Er…"

"Never mind, Thea will sort you out. Thea! Thea! Over here."

The yoga instructor glided over. She had a serene smile on her face and the figure of someone who not only had a well-balanced diet but exercised every day. Fi smiled back, tugging her hair into a wayward ponytail.

"Welcome, welcome. I am Thea, is this your first time?"

"Yes, but…"

"You may borrow one of our mats." She indicated a pile of rolled up mats stacked against a wall. Fi hurried over, grabbed a violet mat and untied the string holding it in place. It sprang open so quickly that Fi jumped back.

"And have you taken a class before?"

"Er, no."

Her brown eyes landed on Cressida. "This is a dog yoga class…"

"I know, but I really wanted to, er, bond with my animal through, er, exercise. We've got a…um…psychic link, and there aren't any wyrm yoga classes."

The yoga teacher raised one eyebrow. "How extraordinary. Try to keep up as best you can, but don't worry if you get lost or need to take it slowly."

The teacher walked away to take her place at the front of the class and Fi went back to struggling to get her mat flat on the ground.

"Do you really have a psychic link with your animal?"

"Yes, yes I do."

"How wonderful. I think that Poppy and I have a connection, sometimes it's as if I know exactly what she's thinking."

Cressida snorted and Fi looked down at the large dog, which was licking its privates. "Hmmm," she said non-commitally. "So, do you have a lot of contact with the spirit world."

"Oh yes," Grace replied eagerly. "Ever since my Pat died, I know he's been trying to contact me. I've been to a couple of psychics you know, but it's so hard to find someone who truly has the gift."

"Yes?"

She nodded. "One old fraud told me that there wasn't any money, but now I see someone much more talented, and we're close to a breakthrough, I can feel it."

Thea coughed and called the class to start in a seated position. Fi moved to a kneeling position with Cressida at the end of the mat. She followed the class as the teacher bent at her waist and reached forward to stroke the basset hound lying calmly at the end of her lime green mat.

Fi twisted her head and whispered, "So, you weren't annoyed with the fraud?"

"Of course, I was! That old bat was lying to everyone, duping poor innocent people, I hate to see that."

"Shhhh." Thea eyed Fi and Grace. Fi followed the next sequence of moves in silence, concentrating on getting herself into a cat then a cow position. After a couple of minutes, she tried again.

"Hate it enough to do something about it?"

"Pardon?"

"The fraud. Did you do something about her?"

"Oh yes."

"Shhhh!"

"And?"

"Fi, I think it would be better if you moved to the front of the class where you can concentrate on your bond with your animal." The yoga teacher interrupted Fi's interrogation.

"I'm fine here, really."

"Nonsense, there's a spot here. Come on, don't be shy."

Cursing inwardly, Fi carried her yoga mat to the place that the teacher indicated. She'd have to wait until the end of the class to get her answers.

Chapter 19

You could try to achieve the pose.

"What does it look like I'm doing?"

I'm sure I don't know.

"You've got it easy, all you have to do is lie there."

After she had stretched and posed in ways she hadn't moved her body in years, the class finally finished. Fi moved back over to Grace and tried to roll up her mat.

"Great session."

"Mmm," Grace agreed, concentrating on her own mat.

"So, you were saying you got back at the psychic you thought was a fraud?"

"What? Oh yes, I left a comment online."

"That's it?"

Grace frowned. "What else should I do? I've found the real deal now, and Sibyl thinks that in only three more sessions I'll be ready to level up to the next stage in the spirit world."

Sounds like a cult.

"Level up?"

"Yes, you see, what happens is that you have the low spirits, that's level one to three, then you get to the middle spirits at level four to eight until I'll get my own high level spirit guide at level nine. That's the equivalent of an angel, or maybe even an archangel. She said I'm getting fast-tracked because I'm so devoted."

Definitely a cult. Ask her if she has to donate money.

"Does this devotion have anything to do with donations?"

"Why, yes, it does. How did you know? You've got a psychic connection, haven't you? How does my aura look to you?"

"Er...I don't know how to say this, but..."

"What? What's the matter? I knew I should have paid for the sage smudging session."

"No, it's not that." Fi took a deep breath and plunged on. "I think you might be in a cult."

Don't sugar coat it.

Fi glared at her familiar as the woman laughed. The wyrm had wanted her to tell Grace what she was involved in.

"A cult? Don't be ridiculous. It's a programme of psychic contact based on the angelic hierarchy and if I show enough dedication and devotion, I'll work up to a seraphim spirit guide and then I'll get to talk to Pat and find out where the money is."

"I just know that Effie told you the truth and..."

126

"Effie? Who's Effie? Wait. You knew that phony, didn't you? What is this?"

"Er…"

"You want me to take down the comment! Well, I won't. Everyone needs to know the truth and I need my money."

"Ladies, there are some negative vibes over here."

"It's alright, Thea, me and Poppy are just leaving." Grace strode out of the room, her mat tucked neatly under her arm and the Labrador lolloping at her side.

Fi stared after her. The mat she held unrolled and fell onto the floor. Fi cursed, apologised to the yoga teacher, and wrestled the mat back into a tight curl before placing it back on the stack.

She fidgeted all the way home, tapping her feet so much that the man next to her on the bus asked her to stop. Back in her room, Fi loaded up her computer and crossed Gracey72 off the suspect list and focused on the teenager. But without a name, there wasn't much she could do. She didn't want to end up on some sort of list by hacking into the local secondary school pupil database.

Frustrated, Fi gave up on her search for the teenager for now and decided to relax with some gaming. She logged in and smiled as she saw that her virtual best friend was online.

Fi-zar: fancy a game?

Adrock: sure. lady's choice

Fi-zar: something with lots of guns

Adrock: tough day at the office?

Fi-zar: something like that

Adrock: want to chat?

Fi-zar: nah, let's shoot something

Chapter 20

Get up.

"Fnah." Fi rolled over and pulled the covers over her head.

Get up!

Fi screwed her eyes closed, hoping the voice would go away. She peeked to see Cressida narrowing her reptilian eyes and, Fi thought, if the wyrm could have pursed her lips, she would have. Instead, she settled for breathing out a small flicker of fire at the wastepaper basket.

The smell of paper burning annoyed the house, which rattled the floor until Fi's bed shook so much that she fell out. After a short exclamation of pain, surprise and annoyance, Fi took the bin through to the bathroom, where she doused it under the tab.

"Happy now?" She waved the bin at the ceiling, but the house stayed quiet. She walked back to her room and glared at the small wyrm. "I'm up."

Good.

"Well?"

You haven't left your room for two days.

"That's not true! I went to the kitchen to get you some coal."

That barely counts. You need some exercise.

Fi shuddered. "I ran through an entire enemy compound last night."

You didn't do that. Your character on the screen did that.

"I went to that yoga class."

That was two days ago.

Fi thought and tried to count back. She had lost herself in a mammoth gaming session, a rarer and rarer occasion as both she and her online friends were getting older, and they had other commitments. One of them even had kids. Maybe she hadn't been outside in forty-eight hours.

You need to take care of your body, come on, I'm taking you for a walk.

"No, don't want to."

Yes.

"Why do you care about my health so much?"

Is it so surprising I care about the health of my witch?

Fi swallowed. Cressida had become so much a part of her life that she often forgot that she had been another witch's familiar before. An older witch with heart problems who had been murdered. She opened her mouth to say something, but Cressida jumped down off the bed.

And make sure you shower. You stink.

Fi started to protest, then sniffed the shirt she had fallen asleep in. OK, maybe she did need to shower. Fifteen minutes later, she tied her long blonde hair back into a ponytail and clipped a lead onto Cressida's collar. She blinked in the late morning sun and pushed a pair of sunglasses over her eyes.

"Lead the way."

Cressida snorted and set off. Her short legs meant that the pace wasn't particularly taxing, and Fi allowed her mind to wander as the golden wyrm took the overgrown footpath outside the house. She replayed the conversation with Adriana over and over in her mind. Something was strange, but Fi had no idea what it was.

The young woman had seemed nice at first, she'd invited Fi to dinner after all, but then had turned cold. Not for the first time, Fi wished she could understand people as well as she could machines. Maybe she should talk to Agatha. Her sister was always the personable one.

And she hadn't found anything else to support her wild theory that Effie had been murdered. Fi had tried to find the goth girl online, but with only a grainy photo and a half-remembered email address to go on, she hadn't got anywhere with that. Inwardly, the tech witch cursed herself for not moving Effie's system onto the cloud before the shop burned down, then she'd have the email address and a name.

She pulled Cressida's lead gently at the next fork in the footpath to indicate that she wanted to go towards the

131

village. Maybe someone there would know who the teenager was.

You can go to town after our walk. I'm not having you cut short the only proper exercise you've had in the past month.

Fi regretted not bringing a mug of coffee with her, but she didn't push it. Walking would always rank behind playing computer games in her life, but it wasn't too bad being outside in the fields that surrounded the country village. It was a perfect spring day, full of promise, with birds calling to each other from the tops of the tall, leafy trees that lined the boundaries, providing shade and white, sweet-smelling blossoms along the route. The occasional creature hopped or flew across the path as the witch and her familiar ambled along.

"Was that a hare?"

If you have to ask if it was a hare, it wasn't a hare.

"What's that supposed to mean?" Fi frowned.

It means it was a rabbit.

"Oh. What's that bird?"

Don't you know anything about the countryside? You live here!

"I suppose I could look it up online..."

Cressida snorted and shook her head. Fi could sense the wyrm's amazement at the strange human she was paired with. The wyrm led the way through a small copse of trees and stopped. She lowered her head to the ground and sniffed.

Fi kept strolling until the lead went taut, oblivious to the small wyrm's change in behaviour.

There's someone up ahead.

Fi tensed. What did that mean? The witch slowed, her power flickering under her skin at the spike in her emotions. "Maybe we should turn back."

Oh no you don't. Come on, Cressida scented the air with her forked tongue. *It's only one female.*

"A female?" Fi shook her head at the dragon-like creature as Cressida carried on walking. She was still jittery after the wyrm's cryptic statement and clutched the lead tightly in her clammy palm, forcing her power down inside her.

They entered a small clearing in the thicket of trees. A few fallen logs had been moved to create a semicircle of seating around burned ground. Empty glass bottles littered the floor. It looked like this was a favourite haunt of local teenagers. Fi remembered coming here once herself, but she hadn't really got the hang of drinking games and had gone home early, back to her online friends who understood her more.

She jolted out of her reminiscence as she spotted a piece of black lace behind a tree. Something about it seemed familiar.

"Hello?" Fi circled round to get a better look. A girl with streaked black makeup stared at her with wide eyes. "Are you alright?"

"I'm fine, just going home." Tears shimmered in the girl's eyes. She stepped out from her hiding place. "You're the witch from the shop, right?"

Fi nodded. "Do you need any help?"

The girl sniffed, then started crying, fat wobbly tears falling down her face. Fi stared helplessly.

Offer her a tissue.

"I haven't got any tissues."

"It's alright, I'd better go anyway…but, if you are a witch, can you put a spell on me?"

"A spell?"

"I need to be invisible. I can't let him find me!"

"Are you being threatened by that boy from the shop? Is that why you ran?"

The girl collapsed onto a mossy log and put her head in her hands.

Chapter 21

Fi sat down next to the girl and patted her shoulder awkwardly. "Do you want to tell me about it?"

"I just…the fire, it was all my fault."

Fi's hand hovered mid-pat. "What do you mean?"

"I did the spell so he could get in."

"Get into the shop?"

The girl nodded, tears spilling from between her fingers.

"Why did he want to get into the shop?"

"George said it would be alright, that no one would get hurt. He'd steal some stock and then the old lady would be able to claim on the insurance. A victimless crime."

"And you helped him get in?" Was this George the figure that Adriana had heard in the shop? Something fluttered in Fi's chest, a feeling that she was on the right track.

"I could sense the wards around the shop, and I told him they were there. He wouldn't even have thought about it if I hadn't said anything. Then I used the spell components he bought and cast a charm so he could get through the protection. But he was meant to do it at night! And, and, I cursed him as well. Oh, what if that, like, totally messed everything up?"

Fi screwed up her face and tried to think. The bag of herbs the boy had bought wouldn't be enough to get him through Effie's powerful wards, even with a witch casting them.

"What do you mean you cursed him?"

"I didn't really want to help him, the old lady was so nice to me about offering to teach me, so I put a small curse on George, just so he wouldn't succeed, and I just wanted him to leave me alone. But it all went wrong!"

"Look…"

"Diane."

"Look Diane, the packet he bought wasn't powerful enough to help anyone get through the shop's wards. Effie was a strong magic user and no offence but you…well…"

"I know, I'm useless. I just thought that maybe I could learn to be a witch, so I could protect myself from boys like George." Diane's shoulders heaved with another sob.

Fi stayed silent. What was there to say? Being a magic user was something you were born with. She'd always thought it was a nuisance at best, a nightmare at worst. She hadn't ever considered that mundane people would actually want to be witches. She paused halfway through a lacklustre pat on the girl's arm.

"Diane, what do you mean, you can sense the wards?"

136

The girl sniffed loudly and met Fi's eyes. "I can see things sometimes, like blurry lines, normally around shops and magical places, like we went to Stonehenge for a school trip a few years ago and I could, like, see the ley lines."

"And do spells you cast normally work?"

The girl's head bobbed up and down eagerly. "Sometimes, like the other day I wanted chips at school, but I was really far back in the queue. So, I focused really hard and when I got to the front, there were still some there!"

Cressida snorted at their feet. Fi kept her expression blank. "OK, I might be able to help. I know a lot of witches. I could ask them to speak to you and assess your power."

"You're in a coven?!" Diane's face brightened and her voice rose half an octave.

Fi leaned back. "More like a family. Anyway, the point is, I can help."

"That would be amazing. Thank you so much. If there's ever anything I can do for you…"

"Actually, I'd like to speak to George."

Diane looked away and stared at a piece of greeny-grey moss on a tree stump. Fi kept quiet. The girl nodded, then pulled out her phone. She tapped at the screen before meeting Fi's eyes.

"He'll be here in an hour."

"Great, thank you."

"I don't want to see him again." The girl's voice was quiet, and her eyes skittered away from Fi to stare at her shoes.

Fi nodded, annoyed at herself for forgetting to think about the girl's feelings. "OK, why don't I take you somewhere safe, and you can talk to my sister about being a witch."

Diane brightened considerably at the promise of meeting another witch. Fi made a quick call and they rushed to the village park. Agatha stood, arms crossed, waiting for them.

"What's this about Fi? This is my day off, and I had a full day of gardening planned."

"Agatha, this is Diane. She thinks she might be a witch."

Agatha smiled warmly at Diane and asked her to sit on a bench with a motherly voice that she'd had since she was a teenager. She made sure the girl wasn't looking, then glared at Fi, opening her mouth to launch into a tirade.

Fi held up her hands. "She can sense wards."

Agatha's anger deflated, and she glanced at the teenager, now swinging her gothic boots as she perched on a bench. "But she's a teenager, has no one noticed before now?"

Fi shrugged. "No idea, but it was either bring her to you or Mum."

Agatha nodded. Both of them could agree that it was better the girl was eased into things rather than confronted with the full force of Nell Blair.

"And she thinks her boyfriend burned down the shop."

Agatha's eyes widened. "So, it wasn't an accident?"

"I don't know, but I don't think so. Have you ever known Effie to leave the cover off her crystal ball?"

138

"Alright, I'll speak to the girl and see what she thinks she can do. But, Fi, be careful, OK?"

"He's a teenage boy, I'll be fine. What's the worst that can happen?" Fi's voice was a little too carefree.

Agatha reached for her hand and squeezed it. "I mean, you tend to latch onto ideas. Just…don't go seeing things that aren't there."

With that, her sister walked away.

She's right, you know, you are single-minded.

"Whose side are you on?"

I'm not on anyone's side. Cressida flicked her tail. *Besides, I didn't say it was a bad thing.*

Fi relaxed a little. "OK, well, if I'm meeting a teenage arsonist in less than an hour, we're going to need to work together."

The small wyrm stared at her.

"I'll get you a fresh bag of coal if you help…" The wyrm blinked but stayed silent. Fi sighed. "And a cut of steak from the butchers."

What did you have in mind?

Chapter 22

Fi waited just off the path until she heard the crunch of twigs and the heavy step that heralded George's arrival. She could tell the exact moment when he noticed that Diane wasn't waiting for him.

"Di? Where are ya?"

Fi stepped forward. George's face scrunched up in confusion.

"Hi, Diane's not here. But I want to talk to you."

He looked her up and down and gave what Fi thought was meant to be a seductive grin. The pimply teenager didn't pull it off. "Sure thing, sexy. Why don't you come closer, and we can get to know each other better?"

Fi groaned. Another idiot who thought he was the goddess' gift to women. "I've got a few questions to ask you." Fi stayed put and forced herself to speak confidently. She would not be cowed by a kid, even if he was taller than her.

"Oh, yeah?" George took a step forward, brazening out his puzzlement.

Fi nodded.

"What's this about?"

"A fire on the High Street…I think you know something about it."

"Really? And even if I did, why would I want to talk to you?" He took another step forward, forcing Fi back as he breached her personal space.

Fi thought about what her sister, the people person would do. Somehow, if Agatha were here, she'd have him sobbing out his life story and telling her everything.

Fi would never have that gift. Her only power was over electricity, and if she didn't do something, this cocky teenager would walk away and she'd never find out whether he killed Effie. The thought of her elderly friend leant Fi determination and she drew a small amount of electricity into her palm. She forced it into a crackling ball that hissed sparks.

George backed off. "Woah, you crazy bitch. I'm off." He turned to leave, and tripped over Cressida who had twined her way between his legs.

Ouch! He trod on my tail! The wyrm hissed.

George tried to scramble away, his lanky limbs making his retreat look awkward.

"Now, now. All I want to do is ask you some questions. Please, take a seat."

George looked longingly at the path. Cressida spit a small burst of flames at him. He nodded quickly and sat down on one of the fallen logs.

Fi stood opposite him.

"Why don't you tell me why you wanted to rob Effie's store?"

"What?"

"The café with the crystals in the village centre."

"Who says I wanted to rob it?"

"George, we can do this the easy way or the hard way." Fi carefully flexed her fingers, making sure only the smallest burst of electricity flashed in her palm. What was her life coming to that she was threatening teenagers? She kept her face blank.

"OK, yeah, maybe I did want to, but I couldn't get in, could I?"

Fi raised an eyebrow.

"Look, I just wanted to get some cash. And some of them fossils can go for a lot online. I figured it would be easy to get in and out. The old bat was away with the fairies most of the time. But Di said there was some sort of magic protection around it." George spat out a gob of phlegm. He wiped his mouth with the back of his hand and carried on. "So, I asked her to do a counter spell but I dunno what happened. Maybe she's not as magical as she thinks. But, it didn't work. I couldn't even get in through the door."

Fi caught herself nodding along. His account matched Diane's. She stopped her head from bobbing. "Why did you try to rob it in the daytime?"

"What? What are you talking about? I'm not stupid." He wiped his nose with the back of his hand. "I wouldn't take anything in broad daylight. Not anything that wouldn't fit in my pocket, anyway."

"So, you didn't set the store alight?"

"That's what this is about?" He laughed and leaned back, confident now. "I wasn't even in town that day. I was hanging with some mates in Swindon."

Fi frowned. "When were you at the shop, then?"

George sniffed and shifted uncomfortably. "I might have checked it out with Diane at night, but the stupid cow ran off. And like I said, I couldn't get in. I didn't do nothing." He ended defiantly, glaring at the witch.

"So, Diane was running across the road to get away from you…"

"Diane! Was it her what told you about this? The stupid bitch! I'll teach her a lesson."

George stood. Fi gulped then stood straighter. She wasn't going to let this idiot get close to Diane again.

"Stop!" she shouted with so much force that the teenager turned to look at her.

Fi allowed her power to arc around them, her hair flew out of its ponytail as the electricity took hold. "You will not go near Diane again. Do you understand?"

As if to reinforce her point, Cressida breathed a fireball that brushed past his shredded denim jeans. He jumped backwards.

"Alright, alright, I won't do nothing!" Panic edged into his voice.

"You will leave Diane alone."

"Yes, yes! I'll leave her alone."

"She's under the protection of the Omensford WWWI. If I hear you've been near her again, there will be consequences."

"I said I'd leave her alone, didn't I?! Let me go!"

Fi forced her power back down. As soon as the swirling blue electricity had disappeared, George legged it out of the clearing.

Very good. 'There will be consequences'. Very threatening.

"OK, I'm not good at threatening people. Do you think he got the message?"

Cressida nodded, her eyes glowing with approval. She snaked her way into Fi's lap and rubbed her head against the witch's chin.

We make a good team.

"We do. Thanks for the assist back there. So," Fi asked the clearing as she absentmindedly stroked the small wyrm, "what do we do now?"

An alarm burst into the quiet of the copse. Fi retrieved her phone from her pocket and stared at it. She swore. Her interview was in twenty minutes.

Chapter 23

Fi arrived back at her family home out of breath and with two minutes to spare. She raced up to her bedroom and tapped her fingers against her thigh as she waited for her computer to load. Cressida curled up on the bed.

You know, if you manage to get a job, you'll have less time to spend chasing mysteries.

Fi ignored the wyrm and opened the meeting invite. The webcam activated. She grimaced and quickly angled it so only the wall was showing rather than the mess of clothes on the floor. She wrestled her frizzy hair into something resembling a ponytail and then checked the rest of her appearance. Frantically, she stripped off her t-shirt and buttoned herself into a white shirt before grabbing a suit jacket. She sat down heavily in her ergonomic chair, dislodging the hoody that she had thrown there. Three minutes late for the interview, she joined the meeting.

At the exact moment that she joined, the hoody landed on the floor with a thump, and something rolled out of the large pocket on the front. Fi winced.

"What was that? Can you hear us OK?" The voice from the screen reminded Fi that she needed to smile.

"Oh, nothing, I just dropped something," she said breezily while her heart pumped with a heady combination of embarrassment and nerves.

"Ah, good afternoon, Miss Blair. I'm Joel Minchin and I'm the interviewer today and this is Lyndsey Saft who's joining us from HR to make sure this is a fair process. Ha, ha. Thank you for coming."

Fi nodded, trying to calm her breathing. "Thank you for agreeing to interview me." Ugh, was that too keen? One hand opened and closed nervously out of sight of the camera.

"Right, well this is a relatively straightforward process. I'll ask you a few questions, then there's a short practical exercise and that's it. I'll be taking notes, so apologies if I don't make eye contact all the time."

"Practical exercise?" Fi squeaked.

"Yes. It was in the invite." Lyndsey narrowed her eyes.

"Right, of course. Yes. Sorry."

Fail to prepare and you prepare to fail, Cressida added from her position on the bed. Fi forced herself to stay focused on the screen.

"Have you got any questions for me before we start?"

146

"Er, no. I don't think so."

"Great. So, tell me, why do you want to be an IT Consultant at GlobalCorpIT?"

"Er, yes. I'm really excited about the opportunity. As you can see from my CV, I've got a lot of experience in the tech industry and I'm keen to make my next move into a firm that covers the entire world."

Joel chuckled. "Well, we're not quite in every country."

Fi kept quiet.

"And you have got a lot of experience in a lot of different companies…"

Fi took a breath to compose herself. She was prepared for this question, she'd had to answer it at every interview since her third role change. "I like to challenge myself and I'm a fast learner. Thanks to my experience, I'm proficient in over twenty different IT systems and in my previous role I was known as the go-to person for any software or hardware issues."

"So, what you're saying is you know IT?" Joel smiled, his dark eyes crinkling at the corners.

Fi nodded. Out of the corner of her eye, she saw Cressida giving her a look that told her she needed to have a better expression.

"And why are you so interested in tech?"

"I guess I caught the bug when I built my first computer when I was ten and ever since then I've been interested in how they work and what programmes they use."

"You programme as well?"

"For myself mostly…" They seemed to expect something more, so she hurried on, "…and I've been providing inventory system support at a local shop for the past few months." Fi stopped.

"Yes, I was going to ask you about that. There's a gap on your CV for the last six months…"

"As I said, I've been focusing on supporting the local community here and implementing a new inventory system." And trying to forget that she'd killed someone.

"How's it operating now?"

"The shop burned down recently…"

"I'm sorry to hear that."

"But before that I was making great strides in cataloguing and improving security." Fi talked quickly, hoping she hadn't blundered too much.

"And whereabouts are you based?"

"Omensford. It's a village in the Cotswolds."

"Oh lovely, I love that part of the world. We were there for a long weekend at Easter."

"Really?" Fi wondered where this was going.

"Yes, near Stow on the Wold, do you know it?"

"It's beautiful."

Joel smiled again. That had been the right response. "And you'll want to be remote based?"

"Er, yes. Unless that's a problem?"

He shook his head. "Not at all, here at GlobalCorpIT, we pride ourselves on our modern work environment. We provide the laptop, and our employees are free to choose where they log in from. We do of course have offices across the UK; London, Bristol, Birmingham, Manchester, Edinburgh – although the commute to Scotland might be a bit far for you." He paused. Was he expecting her to laugh at the feeble joke? She smiled uncertainly and he carried on.

"So, you're welcome to travel in if you get lonely working from home, although not many of our IT team tend to come in much. Ha ha. We also have a companywide sports day once a year. It's a great laugh and a chance to team build."

"The whole company?" Fi frowned, trying to work out the logistics of the global company coming together. There were over ten thousand employees across the world.

Joel laughed. "Just the UK team obviously, the other regions have their own motivation days. We did team up with Europe a few years ago, but Brexit's made that more challenging, so now we mostly keep it to the UK."

"Right. Sounds good."

"It is." He nodded before consulting his notes. "And where do you see yourself in five years' time?"

"Er, in front of my computer screen, solving complex problems."

Cressida rolled her eyes. Joel laughed again and made a note.

"OK, well, that's all my questions. Do you have anything you want to ask me before we start the practical?"

Fi checked the clock. That had been fast. Was that a good or bad thing?

Ask him something.

"Yes, what do you like best about the company?"

"Great question." Joel beamed. "I like the flexibility and the opportunity GlobalCorpIT offers. Really, the sky's the limit."

"As long as you like IT?"

He snorted. "Exactly so. OK, onto the practical. We're going to do a bit of roleplay here. I've got a laptop here with a standard Windows Operating System. Since the latest upgrade, I'm having trouble with it. I want you to try to solve the issue."

"OK, what exactly is the issue?"

"I can't open certain files and the sound keeps cutting out in meetings."

"Have you tried turning it off and on again?"

Joel smiled and nodded.

"OK, it's probably best if I take a look. Can I remote login?"

"Absolutely, the details are in the meeting invite. I should point out that this is a standalone laptop for interviews, you won't be able to access our systems at all, only what's on the laptop."

Fi tapped her keyboard quickly. "OK, you should have a pop up on the screen now. If you click OK, I'll be able to see exactly what's going on."

Joel nodded and followed her instructions. Fi relaxed. This was her bread and butter. She enjoyed the puzzle of a new computer, seeing everything, getting an understanding of its workings. Her power hummed in response to the technology. She forced it back. She wasn't going to blow up this computer and literally blow the interview. After a minute of digging around, Fi thought she had the answer.

"I'm going to recommend a complete re-installation, and then I'd like to check the sound drivers again." Joel nodded along and took notes. "It also looks like there's a virus in the system. I'm going to uninstall that file now and then you can do the update."

"A virus?" Joel checked his paperwork. "There's no virus."

"Yep, I'm afraid you've got a password scraper going on in the background. Here, see this CPU usage?" Fi brought up the screen.

Joel studied it. His face blanched. "That's not supposed to be there!"

"Uh, do you want me to get rid of it for you?"

"Um, um, yes?" His voice cracked.

"OK, give me a minute...." Fi uninstalled the file and double checked it wasn't sitting anywhere else on the computer. "There. All done. How do you want me to do the re-installation of the operating system? Normally I'd push everything from the in-house IT system but obviously I'm not in-house...do you want me to use the standard update?"

"Um, yes, please." Joel scribbled furiously.

Fi completed the task and waited patiently.

"Right, well thanks Ms Blair. We'll be in touch." Joel ended the call abruptly.

Fi stared at the screen.

That went well.

"You think so?"

I don't even think he noticed your buttons were askew.

Fi looked down and cursed as she realised that the collar button was out of alignment. A glint of light caught her eye. She bent down and retrieved the item that had fallen from her hoody in her scrabble to get ready. It was the crystal that Effie had given her.

Chapter 24

She looked at the round crystal from every angle. It was a strange purplish-blue colour, polished to a high shine. Very different from the tiger's eye gemstones she owned – relics from her misguided teenage years when she had thought they might help her control her magic.

She held it up to her eye, her room refracted in strange angles through the crystal.

What is it?

"No idea. Effie gave it to me. Maybe Mum knows."

Fi wandered downstairs to find her mother. She was so distracted, she almost collided with Adriana coming upstairs.

"Sorry."

Adriana smoothed down her pleated, red dress. "Watch where you're going." She looked the witch up and down. Fi instinctively palmed the crystal and held it behind her back.

"Where are you going in such a hurry, anyway?"

"Just needed to see Mum, I had my job interview just now so…"

Adriana's eyes narrowed, but she smiled. "How did it go?"

"Oh, you know..." Fi edged her way past the young woman.

"Did you know your buttons are out of line?"

"Are they? Thanks for telling me. Anyway, better go." She hurried to the kitchen, glancing back as she reached the door to see Adriana staring after her and tapping her chin with one finger. She caught Fi's eye and gave a fake smile before heading to her room.

Something's wrong with that woman. Cressida looked back before following Fi through into the kitchen.

Fi sighed as she shut the wooden kitchen door and leant against it.

Her mother was in the kitchen, tending to a strong-smelling potion brewing on the aga. Fi scrunched up her nose.

"What is that smell?"

"Plant food. I'm trying a new recipe; I think I might have overdone the ammonia."

Fi nodded and tried to breathe through her mouth. Her throat burned.

Nell glanced at her daughter. "Your buttons are askew."

Fi rolled her eyes and redid her shirt buttons.

"How did your interview go?"

"I'm not sure, but I solved a virus issue for them, so..." She shook her head. "Anyway, I didn't want to talk about interviews. I wanted to talk about this." Fi looked around to make sure they were alone before opening her hand to reveal the small crystal.

Nell squinted. "What is it?"

Fi's shoulders slumped. "I thought you might know."

"Come here and let me have a closer look."

Fi held her breath and walked towards her mother and the pungent potion. Nell took the crystal from her.

"Hmmm, it's some sort of crystal."

"I know that!"

"Unusual colouring and a strong magical affinity. And you don't know what it is?"

Fi shook her head.

"Where did you find it?"

"Effie gave it to me, just before…"

Nell met her daughter's eyes. "Well, we'd better find out what it is, then." Without another word, she turned off the stove, abandoned her potion and led the way to the library.

Fi inhaled the familiar scent of paper and lemon polish, refreshing after the stench in the kitchen. The two witches walked past leather-bound books and a shelf full of scrolls, which rustled slightly as they rearranged themselves.

Nell studied the polished stone again. "Did she say anything when she gave it to you?"

Fi screwed up her face as she thought, then she shook her head. "She just said to keep it away from Adriana and something about it giving you whatever you want." Fi's face drained of colour. "Oh goddess, do you think she can sense it?"

Nell pursed her lips, considering, "The house's magic might dampen the feel of it. I didn't notice anything magical about it until I held it. Why did Effie want to keep it from her great-niece, though? That is the question. Well, we'd better see if we can find out more about it."

The elder witch returned the crystal to Fi then clapped her hands together. "We need information about this crystal. Please."

A rustling of pages built up as the house considered the request. A shudder went round the library before two books moved an inch out of their shelves. Nell grabbed them and murmured her thanks to the house before settling herself on the large Chesterfield sofa and flicking through the pages of a weighty tome on minerals.

Fi joined her and picked up the slimmer book titled *Crystals and Their Uses*. She skimmed over the pages, but none of the pictures matched the ethereal looking stone that now sat on the low coffee table.

This is pointless, Cressida sulked as she prodded the crystal with one clawed foot.

"Is this all we've got on crystals?"

Nell nodded. "It must be, or the house would have selected some more. Maybe we're looking at this the wrong way...perhaps it's a magic artefact." Nell stood again and closed her eyes as she thought about the stone.

Fi reached for her phone. If the magical house library couldn't help, perhaps the internet would hold the answers. She searched for crystals, crystal balls and artefacts. Nothing useful came up. But the house took Fi's searches as an affront to its inbuilt knowledge and responded by shuddering more books out of the tightly packed shelves. One of them hit the floor.

"Alright, alright," Fi muttered as she went to retrieve it. She swallowed as she saw the tattoo inked on its leathery spine; she had never opened a volume bound in human skin before. She pushed down the squeamish bubble that rose in her stomach, grabbed the book from the floor and headed back to the table.

Nell picked up the others and they settled down to look. Some of the books contained obscure references to artefacts, others to famous crystal balls.

"I think I might have something…" Nell put down a slim book on the coffee table, its ochre-coloured bindings standing out against the wooden surface.

Fi put down the grisly book she had in her hands on top of a copy of *Exciting Rocks of Our Times* and bent over to study the illustration. It bore some resemblance to Effie's crystal, but the picture was faded. Fi read the text next to it.

"It shows the thing you most desire…what does that mean?"

Nell picked up the crystal and stared at it. Fi held her breath. After long moments, she let it out again. Nothing happened.

"Maybe it's attuned to Effie." Nell glared at the artefact as if it had personally betrayed her by not doing anything.

"Or maybe it's nothing."

Chapter 25

Fi headed back upstairs with a sandwich and a lump of coal for Cressida. Her mother has tsked at her eating alone but had been too distracted by feeding her garden the stinky potion to insist that Fi eat with her. She placed the crystal on her desk next to her faithful laptop. She ate her sandwich slowly, staring at the gemstone. Her phone rang.

"Hello?"

"Hi Fi, how'd it go?"

"Oh, hi Mort, how did what go?"

"The interview? It was today, right?"

"Oh, yeah. OK, I think."

"Are you alright? You sound a bit distracted."

"No, yeah, I'm fine."

"Do you want me to come over?"

"No, no. I'm fine." The silence on the end of the phone was deafening. "Really. I'm fine. I'll talk to you later. OK?"

"If you're sure…"

"I'm sure. Bye Mort and, er, thanks for calling."

She hung up. A text buzzed through. She frowned and opened it. Maxi had sent her a picture of himself in front of dark clouds and a message: *Storm's coming, thinking of you.*

She flung her phone down on the bed. Another reference to her dangerous power. Was that all she was?

Impulsively, she pushed herself up and snatched up the crystal. She stared into its swirling centre.

"Alright then, show me what I want," she demanded. It stayed blank. She shook her head and made to throw it down, but a slight movement caught her eye. She frowned. The centre clouded over, and an image appeared. For a second, it showed Fi, sitting at a desk, talking to someone on a headset. Then Maxi's familiar face swam into view with his mad professor hair. She couldn't help but smile. Then Maxi disappeared and Mort came into focus, his eyes so caring it hurt her to look at the picture. Mort faded and Adriana filled the crystal.

"What?" Fi gaped at the crystal. Did she want to date Adriana?

The image of the young woman in her neat red dress resolutely filled the stone. Fi closed her mouth and studied it more closely. She stood amidst rubble, poking at the dirt with a high-heeled shoe.

And a crazy thought entered Fi's head. The one thing she wanted most was to figure out who had killed Effie. She raced back downstairs.

"Come on, Cressy, we're heading out."

160

Chapter 26

A short while later, Fi walked through the charred entryway to Effie's café. There was no light inside, and the darkening skies shed a gloomy light on the shop's carcass. A flash of red drew her attention.

"Hello."

"Oh, hello."

"What are you doing here?" Fi looked around the skeleton of the burned shop.

"I just wanted to be near her." Adriana's voice was breezy. Too breezy. She drummed her long fingers against the burnt counter. "What are *you* doing here?"

Fi ignored her question. "One thing's been puzzling me, *Adriana*, you've only been here for a couple of days, but you know all about me moving back in with Mum and you love Sorella's? How do you know so much about Omensford?"

The young lady flicked a speck of dust from her bright dress.

"You know what I'm talking about. And you said you're a vegan, but you love steak. What is going on?" Fi pressed on.

"Ah." Adriana looked up at the burned ceiling, then back down to the dusty floor.

Fi waited. Outside, raindrops began to beat down on the pavement.

The young woman sighed. "I suppose you wouldn't believe me if I told you that it was intuition."

Fi shook her head. "I saw something interesting when I looked into the crystal Effie gave me. I wanted to know what had happened to her, and it kept showing me your face."

"And you think I killed her?"

Fi nodded.

Adriana's shoulders sagged. When she spoke, her voice sounded older. "What if I told you I *was* her?" She added a dramatic swirl of her hands.

Fi's eyes widened at the gesture, so like Effie. Cressida tilted her head up and snapped her tail.

That's what I sensed with her magic, it was like Effie's when you spoke in the hall, but then it changed.

"What?" Fi's brain couldn't keep up.

"Figured it out, have you?" Adriana's voice turned cold as if she was a different person.

Fi's brain raced. There was only one possible answer, but it didn't make any sense.

162

"I killed her and now you will give me the crystal, or I will kill you too." Adriana's face twisted into a smirk at Fi's confusion.

Fi blinked at the rapid change in personality. And what did she mean about being Effie?

"Where is the crystal? I won't ask again." Bright balls of shimmering white light appeared in Adriana's palms. "Three...two..." Adriana doubled over, grabbing her stomach. "No! Fi, you have to run! I don't know if I can...ugh...hold her."

Fi backed up, still not understanding. "What's going on?"

"It's me, Effie, but...I can't...she's strong..." The young woman's voice changed again. "You should have run while you had the chance!"

Flee, you moron!

Chapter 27

Cressida darted at Adriana's leg and clamped her teeth around her calf. Disgust roiled through Fi and she shook her head. Where had that emotion come from?

Adriana screamed and aimed a bolt of light at the wyrm. Cressida yelped and fell to the ground with a thud. Fi screamed as pain lanced through her own body. What was happening? Could she sense Cressida's feelings?

"Hold on, Cress," she muttered, trying to sense her familiar through her bond, but the brief flash of emotion and pain was gone.

Adriana kicked the wyrm's body to one side, gathered light to her hands and aimed a blast at Fi. Fi dived to one side. Her knee connected with the ground hard, followed by her thigh. She felt her own power crackling just below her skin and drew it to her fingers. She let off a bolt of electric energy at Adriana. The young woman shrieked as it singed her arm.

"Stupid witch! Just tell me where the crystal is!"

Fi looked around desperately. She saw something glint under the rubble. She scrambled backwards until her hand closed around something round. Fi clutched it in her palm and stood up. Pain blossomed in her leg. She stumbled. Adriana moved towards her, magic glowing in her palms.

"Wait!" Fi shouted. "This is what you want." She opened her hand to reveal a small, perfectly round transparent crystal ball.

Adriana took a step forward.

"Ah, ah." Fi shook her head and turned her palm so it faced the floor. "One more step and I'll smash it."

"You wouldn't!"

"Want to try me?" Fi fumbled with the ball.

"No! Alright, alright. What do you want?" Adriana shook her hands, getting rid of the power gathered there.

"I want to speak to Effie."

Adriana grimaced and closed her eyes. She opened them again. "Fi?"

"Effie, is it really you?"

The young woman nodded, and Fi searched her face, looking for any familiar lines or expression. Was that Effie in the slight crinkle by her eye or the tilt of her head?

"Tell me how to help you."

"Yes, you just have to give me the crystal and I'll be able to take control of the body fully." She smiled broadly and took a step closer to Fi.

165

"That's what I thought you'd say." Fi backed away and let the crystal fall to the ground. It smashed.

"No! What did you do that for?"

Fi backed away towards the door. "Nice try, Adriana, but the real Effie would know that wasn't the crystal you're looking for." She was unable to resist mimicking the Star Wars line even as Adriana stalked forward.

"Tell me where it is!" Adriana's hair blew around her face. She clenched her fists and released a blast of light into Fi's chest. Fi screamed as the light burned through her clothes and into her skin.

A blur of gold darted across the room and latched onto the witch's leg. Adriana screamed and kicked out, sending Cressida flying over the rubble. Fi cried out and clutched her chest, feeling the pain as her familiar hit the ground with a dull thud.

"No!" Adriana screamed and collapsed in on herself as Effie took control of the body again. She looked up at Fi. "Do it! You have to stop her! Use your power."

Fi lifted her arm, tears filling her eyes as she pointed at the body that housed her friend. Then she dropped her arm with a sob. She couldn't do it. Couldn't kill someone else.

Effie's eyes changed and Adriana launched herself at Fi. The tech witch willed all of her power to her fingers. Her hair stood on end as the electrical current flowed through her. She loosed a bolt of lightning directly at the hunched witch. Adriana, or possibly Effie, screamed and fell to the ground.

"I'm sorry, Effie," Fi panted as she fought to control the pain in her chest that consumed her consciousness. She fumbled her phone out of her pocket and unlocked it with her thumbprint. She called the first name in her phone book, her vision swimming in and out of focus.

"Aggy," she whispered, "I'm hurt."

"Goddess! Fi, where are you?" Her sister's voice ramped up in panic.

"Shop. Effie, she…she's alive."

"Oh Fi, I'll be there as soon as I can. Listen to my voice, don't fall asleep whatever you do! Neville! Watch Bea, Fi's hurt! Fi, are you still there? I'm coming…"

Fi closed her eyes and listened to her sister ramble her way out of the front door and into the car before she drifted into the blissful release of unconsciousness.

Chapter 28

"What happened?"

"I don't know. I was on my way to see Fi when I saw a lightning bolt fly out of the shop. I came in and both of them were on the floor. What are you doing here?"

"Fi said she was in trouble…"

Fi fought her way to consciousness. The first thing she registered was the pain in her chest. She groaned.

"Fi, it's alright. I'm here. I've called an ambulance."

Fi looked up into Mort's caring face and shook her head. "Adriana…"

"Adriana did this to you?"

"I didn't even know she was a witch," Agatha chimed in as she bent her head to look more closely at her sister.

Fi tried to push herself up, gritting her teeth against the hot pain in her chest.

"Don't worry, just rest."

"No. No!" Fi struggled into a seated position. "She killed Effie…and Cressida! Where's Cressida?"

"Shhh, you're getting agitated."

"Where is that ambulance?" Agatha got up and looked out of the shop window.

"Effie told me…"

"You saw a ghost?"

"No!" Fi scrunched up her hands in frustration. "She is Effie…" Her words disappeared into a groan as pain jolted through her body.

"You're not making any sense, Fi."

"Oh, thank goddess, they're here. Over here! Over here!"

Fi kept her eyes trained on Adriana's prone body as the paramedics took her pulse and hooked her up to an IV before getting her onto the stretcher. She tried to stay awake, but the quiet hum of the ambulance motoring to the Great Western Hospital in Swindon lulled her to sleep.

Chapter 29

She woke up in a bed wearing a standard hospital gown.

"Where are my clothes?" Fi croaked out the first thought that came into her head.

Her mother sat by the side of her bed and poured her a glass of water. After she had helped Fi drink, Nell lifted the transparent bag a member of staff had given her.

Fi blinked as the bag swam in and out of focus. "Did they cut off my clothes?"

Nell nodded. "And really Fi, that's the underwear you choose to wear? It doesn't even match!"

"What? I should have expected this sort of thing to happen?!"

"No," her mother sighed. "Of course not. I just...I'm worried about you."

It was about the closest that Nell ever came to an apology. Fi reached out and laid her hand over her mother's.

Suddenly, the formidable Nell Blair seemed older. "Sorry, Mum."

Nell covered Fi's hand with her own and squeezed slightly. "You have nothing to be sorry for."

Agatha peeked through the curtains before entering with two cups of tea.

"The tea bag's still in," Nell complained.

"Sorry Mum, I wanted to get back as quickly as possible."

Nell rooted around in her handbag and handed her daughter a green glass bottle. "Drink this."

Fi took the familiar Cure All and lifted it slowly to her lips, wincing as lifting her arms pulled on her chest wound. Nell reached over to help. Fi took a large gulp before Agatha snatched the bottle away. She grimaced at the overpowering aniseed flavour. The pain lessened from agonising to awful.

"Mum! I'm not sure that potion should be mixed with the pain medication!"

"Nonsense, it's fine, it'll help speed things up. I don't know why they don't stock it in the pharmacy here." Nell paused. "Maybe I should speak to somebody about it…"

"I don't think the medical professionals are going to want your advice, Mum."

"Where's Cressida? And Adriana? Did she…? Is she…?" Fi cut across their conversation.

Agatha and Nell exchanged a look. "We left the wyrm with Neville. She's fine, just shaken. But Adriana's still unconscious. The doctors aren't saying anything but…"

Fi let out a sigh of relief and her shoulders relaxed. She hadn't killed anyone...yet. "We can't let her die! She's Effie!"

Another look passed between Fi's sister and mother. "She's not Effie, dear."

Fi rubbed her forehead and winced as the canula in her arm pulled against her skin. "I'm not crazy! Somehow Effie was in Adriana's body with Adriana. She tried to kill me, but Effie stopped her."

"I know that's what you said happened and nobody's disagreeing with you."

"But you don't believe me." Fi looked at them accusingly.

"You're getting agitated!"

"Because no one believes me! I want to talk to Liv."

"Liv?"

Fi nodded and crossed her arms tightly over her chest, screwing her face up at the grating scratch of the bandages over her raw chest and the twinge of the needle in her arm. "She's a shrink. She can go into my subconscious and tell you I'm not lying."

"Dr De'ath is here." Agatha changed the subject.

"Mort?"

"He's been waiting outside ever since you were brought in…"

Fi tapped her fingers against her arm as she thought. Why had he waited? He was a nice person, and a medical professional. That would be it. But somehow the thought

172

that he'd waited to make sure she was OK warmed her insides and made her tummy do a strange flip. She nodded. She wanted to see him. Agatha went outside and re-entered moments later with the doctor at her side.

A nurse called out. "Only two visitors to a bed!"

"Alright, alright, we'll leave you two in privacy."

Fi looked around the ward. The woman in the next bed lifted a hand and waved at her. Even with the modesty curtain, private was not a word that could accurately be used to describe an NHS hospital ward.

"We should check on Adriana anyway..." Agatha led Nell away.

Fi narrowed her eyes after them and clamped her mouth shut. The more she protested that Adriana was a murderer or somehow had two people in her body, the crazier she seemed.

"How are you feeling?" Mort read the clipboard hung at the end of the bed.

"Doesn't that tell you how I am?"

"No. This tells me what's wrong with you. I asked how you're feeling."

"I feel like I've been blasted in the chest."

"Is that all?"

Fi's lips twitched.

"Do you want to talk about it?"

She shrugged but didn't say anything.

"I saw Adriana's charts too..."

173

Fi looked at him with renewed interest.

"It looks like she was struck by lightning, and she has serious burns, much like you..."

Fi shifted guiltily.

"Do you want to tell me what happened?"

She bit her lip then shrugged again, might as well get it over with and have someone else think she was mad. "Adriana attacked me with some sort of burning light when I tricked her into revealing she wasn't Effie, and I used my electrical magic and it went wrong, like always, and now she's dying and it's all my fault that Effie's dying...again."

Mort reached for her face and turned her head gently until she met his warm, brown eyes. "Adriana had a cardiac incident but she's recovering well, medically speaking. In fact, everyone's surprised she's not already awake...I know you wouldn't have used your power if she hadn't forced you. You were defending yourself. It wasn't your fault."

He held her gaze until Fi gave a slight nod. She might not believe him, but maybe it was a first step to accepting her power.

"Now, do you want to tell me why you think Effie is dying again?"

Fi looked away and took a deep breath. "Adriana killed Effie; she told me herself but somehow Effie's spirit was inside her as well. Effie stopped Adriana from killing me, but she couldn't hold her so I...I electrocuted her." She sighed. "I know you won't believe me but that's what happened."

Mort nodded slowly. "I believe you."

"You do?" Fi's mouth opened wide.

"I've seen it before."

Chapter 30

Fi leaned forward. "What? When?"

Mort opened his mouth. The curtains rustled. Agatha slunk in sideways through the gap.

"Fi, you won't believe this! Mum thinks Adriana's a witch." Fi raised one eyebrow as Agatha barrelled on. "Her power is building, but while she's unconscious, she can't control it or channel it anywhere. We've got to wake her up before the power build up becomes critical."

"What happens when it becomes critical?" Mort asked.

Agatha shuddered. "Nothing good."

"How are you planning on waking her up?"

"No idea. Mum asked the doctors to use the defibrillator, but they refused, and Mum's been escorted from the hospital! I think she thought that another shock might wake Adriana up…" Agatha looked meaningfully at Fi.

"Oh no, I don't want to risk losing control and blowing up part of the hospital."

"If you don't, the whole ward might be destroyed anyway when her power becomes too much. I'm going back now to work up a containment spell, but who knows how long we have."

"There must be another way of waking her up...Liv!"

Agatha narrowed her eyes. "Is this about you thinking that she's really Effie?"

Fi fidgeted with the bedsheet.

"I knew it! Come on, Fi! Whoever heard of someone being two people?"

"It can happen," Mort interjected quietly.

"What?"

"Multiple souls can live in one body. It's sometimes misdiagnosed as a number of psychological illnesses because it's so rare. But it happens."

"Like Multiple Personality Disorder?" Agatha frowned, trying to understand.

"That's a real illness, but yes, something like that."

"So, Effie could really be in Adriana's body?"

Mort nodded.

"Then we have to try to get her back." Fi pushed herself up. The pain medication must have kicked in, because the blazing fire in her chest was down to a low burn.

Agatha shook her head. "You are not doing anything. I will call Liv and set up the containment spell. You can rest."

Fi looked at Mort for support.

"Sorry Fi. I'll go talk to the doctors, maybe I can get Adriana moved to a private room in case anything goes wrong."

Fi sank back against the bed and watched them leave. She tapped her fingers against her thigh a few times and fiddled with the television set attached to the wall by a metallic arm. It refused to turn on, so she gave up. She huffed out a breath and looked around the ward. No-one paid her any attention.

Most of the patients' faces were backlit with the blue-white glow from their phones. Two people had visitors. The lady in the bed next to hers flipped a page in a dog-eared romance novel. Fi could see her through the small gap between the faded blue curtains around her bed. The lady looked up, caught Fi's eye and gave a small nod of acknowledgement. From the dull pain in her injured leg, Fi realised her foot was tapping along with her fingers. Time to do something.

She pushed herself upright. It took longer than she wanted thanks to the intense pain in her chest whenever she changed position and the intermittent sharp discomfort every time she moved her arm and the canula pulled under her skin. Long minutes later, she was standing. She shuffled forward, using her bed to help her move along.

The lady in the bed next to hers lifted her head, tucking a stray lock of hair behind her ear. "Loo's over there."

"Thanks, but I'm getting out of here."

"A jail break? How exciting!" She abandoned her novel and studied Fi.

"Not exactly," Fi muttered. She concentrated on placing one foot in front of another, slowly making her way out of the ward. Once she was in the corridor, she paused, scanning the signs for a lift.

"Can I help you?" A nurse sitting behind a large, curved counter peered at Fi.

"Yes, I'm looking for Adriana Harrington. I think she's been moved to a private ward. We're friends."

The nurse narrowed her eyes and tapped something into a screen. Her expression softened. "You were in an accident together today?"

Fi nodded. So, they were calling it an accident.

"She is in the hospital, but I can't give you her room number. And you should be resting! Here, let me help you back to your bed."

Fi began to protest but the nurse had already moved to her side. A loud crash echoed around the corridor. The nurse scanned the ward and saw one of the patients on the floor next to a metallic bedpan and a toppled side cupboard. She rushed over to help. Fi stared.

It was her next-door neighbour in the ward. Her novel lay on the floor where it had fallen. The nurse pulled the woman back onto her bed before pressing a button to call for a doctor. The lady met Fi's eyes and winked before closing her eyes and moaning softly. A young doctor raced down the corridor, ignored Fi and headed for the collapsed patient.

Fi shuffled behind the counter and scanned the screen. Certain she had the room number memorised, she headed on to the lifts. She felt her power leaping under her skin in response to the adrenaline of eluding the nurse and fought to keep it under control. A spark jumped from her finger as she pressed the button to call the elevator. With a shudder, the light on the call button went out. Fi swore. She jabbed the button a few more times. No response. She had shorted the lift. With another curse word on her lips, she headed for the stairs. She clutched at the banister and slowly headed down to the second floor.

She counted to a hundred as she inched down the stairs, focusing on the numbers instead of the all-consuming pain. An age later, she swayed to a stop outside the room. Two doctors and a nurse rushed past, shouting something about a pregnant lady stuck in a lift. Fi winced. That was her fault.

She peeked through the glass. Agatha swirled her hands in complicated patterns as she worked the containment spell. Mort stood to one side, watching with interest. A hot stab of jealousy bubbled in Fi's chest. She pushed it away. Now was not the time to pine over a potential boyfriend and her sister was devoted to her accountant husband, for reasons that Fi couldn't fathom.

A hand touched her shoulder. Fi jumped, then shrieked as the pain in her chest flared.

"Sorry, didn't mean to scare you. What are you doing down here?"

Fi smiled. It took some effort and looked more like a grimace. "Hi Liv, I …"

"You wanted to see the show?"

Fi's shoulders slumped and she nodded. Was she so obvious?

"Better come in then." Liv transferred the wicker basket she held to her other hand and offered her arm to Fi. Together, the two witches entered the room.

Chapter 31

Fi panted as she burst into the room. She could feel the power radiating in waves from the prone young woman on the bed. Liv was much calmer. Fi envied her friend her cool, calculated way of assessing things. While the tech witch had to force herself to stay still, Liv radiated a reassuring presence that made one want her to take charge and solve all your problems. Fi guessed that was why she was such a good therapist. Agatha finished the containment spell with a flourish and the waves calmed to ripples.

Fi collapsed onto the single chair in the room. Mort rushed over and checked her pulse. She smiled up at him, his fingers cool against the throbbing heat of her skin.

Agatha pulled Liv into a hug before stepping back and looking at her expectantly.

"So, talk me through this again. You garbled a lot on the phone, and all I know is that I had to rearrange my last appointment to be here and that wasn't easy." Liv looked at Agatha.

"Thanks for coming. Adriana here is unconscious, and her power is surging dangerously. The doctors don't know how to wake her up, but if she doesn't, the explosion of pent-up power could destroy part of the hospital."

"Can't you shock her awake?" Liv raised one perfectly shaped eyebrow in Fi's direction.

Fi made to get up, but Agatha stepped between her and Liv. "Look at her, she's in no state to practice magic and…she might, you know…"

"Kill her?" Fi supplied.

"Hurt yourself, I was going to say. Your power is volatile."

Fi hung her head. It was true.

Liv studied the young woman lying in the bed, hooked up to a beeping machine and guarded by two rails to make sure she couldn't accidentally fall off her mattress. "So, you want me to enter her unconscious mind and try to bring her back."

"You're the best at what you do." Agatha smiled winningly.

"There's more." Fi interjected from the chair, pushing Mort aside as he shone a small torch into her eyes and studied her pupils. She tried to stand, but Mort gently pressed on her shoulder. She glared at him before turning back to Liv. "Effie's inside her."

Liv raised her other eyebrow at the tech witch. Fi held her gaze.

"Somehow Effie and Adriana are both in there." She hooked a thumb towards the bed.

Liv looked between the three conscious people in the room.

"It's…possible." Mort met her gaze.

"I've never had to locate two people in the dream world before…" She frowned.

"If anyone can do it, you can." Agatha reached out and squeezed her hand.

"Anything else I should know?"

"I want to come with you." Mort stood.

All eyes turned to the tall doctor.

"What do you mean?" Liv didn't quite snap at him, but it was close.

"If there are two souls vying for one body, it means that something has gone wrong. I want to come with you. I can help."

Fi looked up at the doctor with wide eyes, but it was Liv who spoke. "What do you mean, you can help?"

Mort sighed and rubbed his forehead with one hand. Fi reached out and patted his other hand, still resting on her shoulder.

"My surname is De'ath." The women nodded. "It's not just a surname." He looked around at the faces, crinkled with confusion. "Eons ago, when the Lord of the Underworld walked the earth, he chose a family to help him. Not to kill people, but to help make sure that the gates of the underworld stay shut and that souls stay at peace."

"At peace?" Liv echoed.

184

Mort nodded. "Where they belong. There used to be a big problem with restless souls causing mayhem in the mortal realm. It's where a lot of myths come from. Nowadays, it doesn't happen often, but when it does, my family gets involved."

"Why aren't you finding Effie's soul, then?" Fi asked, still trying to grapple with his news. He didn't mention this over curry, but then, maybe it wasn't a first date conversation.

"If I could, I would. But when there are two souls and one body it's more complicated. I think that Liv's powers combined with mine can help."

Liv smoothed the front of her pastel suit. "Alright then, let's do this."

She took out a large tartan blanket from the wicker basket she carried and laid it on the floor.

"Can we do anything to help?" Agatha straightened a corner of the blanket, then hovered between the rug and the hospital bed.

Liv shook her head. "I'm going to enter the dream realm and try to contact Adriana and Effie. I need something of hers."

Agatha rooted around the small bedside cupboard and emerged holding a stiletto shoe triumphantly. Liv raised an eyebrow but took it without comment.

"Mort, lie next to me and hold my hand; it will make it easier for us to connect in the subconscious. I should warn you all that even with one consciousness, there's no guarantee that I can make contact or bring them back. And finding two without a proper tether or connection is uncharted territory for me."

"And you can keep Mort with you in the other realm?"

Liv shot Fi a megawatt smile. "Honey, you know I can dreamwalk with people, we used to do it all the time when we were kids."

Fi didn't know if that was reassuring or not. Liv had led them to the dream realm many times during teenage sleepovers, but there was that one time...with the dark forest, and the ravens, and something behind them, chasing. Just out of sight but getting ever closer. She gripped Mort's hand more tightly and couldn't stop the shiver that ran through her body.

"What should we do while you're gone?" Agatha asked, unaware of Fi's mounting terror.

"Make sure no one interrupts me and keep her magic contained. I do not want to be here if the hospital blows up."

Agatha nodded. "Got it."

"Are you sure it's safe?" Fi blurted out.

Liv met her blue eyes and Fi knew that she had instantly read the true meaning behind her question. Sometimes having a therapist for a friend was a good thing. She bent down and held Fi's hand. "I will do everything in my power to keep him safe."

Fi's cheeks heated and she shook her head, her long white-blonde hair moving wildly around her face. Liv squeezed her hand before laying down on the blanket. Fi blinked away the fuzzy tears that filled her eyes and wondered why Liv had even bothered to bring a rug; it did practically nothing to soften the hard vinyl floor. It didn't even look like a bed.

Liv looked up at Mort from her spot on the floor and patted the soft tartan. He got down awkwardly and lay ramrod straight next to her.

"It's important that you empty your mind."

He nodded, his jaw clenched. Liv took his hand and his face relaxed, although a faint frown line remained between his eyebrows.

"You have to empty your mind. Even better if you can sleep…"

Agatha jumped forward. "I think I have a sleeping potion somewhere in here." She frantically rummaged in her bag. Mort half sat up, ready to take the proffered potion.

Liv shook her head. "That won't work. Sleeping potions dull the subconscious, they don't allow people to dream, and I need a dream state. We'll do this another way."

"Keep your eyes closed and listen to my voice. You are completely relaxed…" Liv kept her voice calm and unhurried as she worked through the hypnosis. Fi felt her own panting breaths become steadier; Liv was that good. Fi watched closely as, Mort's breathing steadied into a rhythmic pattern and his jaw relaxed. Fi wanted to look away, it felt too personal seeing him asleep, so vulnerable, but she couldn't help herself as she studied his face. Liv caught Fi's eye and gave her a wink before closing her own eyes and slipping off to sleep, or wherever it was that the dream witch disappeared to.

187

Chapter 32

Mort spun round. He was in a meadow of thigh-high silver-green grass that looked like nothing he had ever seen. Movement caught his eye and he stumbled back, his mouth falling open as an enormous lion with a flowing pink mane and darker reddish wings flew overhead. A copper-coloured unicorn charged past, shaking its head as it raced the flying lion.

Golden griffins and slender purple dragons played in the pastel blue sky, skirting around small fluffy clouds and leaving trails of sparkling magical glitter. He took another step backwards, crushing flowers beneath his feet. A strange sweet smell, like peppermint and toffee combined wafted up, calming him as he focused on fluffy sheep bouncing over a wooden gate. So this was the dream realm.

"Wow!"

Liv smiled at him. He gazed around her oasis of calm with awe, staring at a flowing dream dragon that undulated through the sky.

She reached out and took his hand. "Come on, we've got to find Adriana...and Effie." Her brow crinkled.

"Try Adriana first, it's her body after all," Mort suggested, unable to tear his eyes from the twisting dragon.

Liv closed her eyes and her forehead puckered, then the meadow dissolved and a maze formed in its place.

Huge dark hedges reached for the sky, which swirled in dark crimson and black overhead. Confusing shadows fell on the sandy ground. Liv sighed next to him. He turned his head.

"What is this place?" Mort whispered, not wanting to break the deep silence of the maze.

"A typical dream. At a glance, I'd say the hedge maze represents confusion and a sense of being lost."

Mort stared at her.

Liv shrugged. "I'm a sleep therapist and a dream witch. Bad dreams come with the territory."

"So, do we go in?"

Liv squared her shoulders. "We go in."

They travelled through the first three turns in the maze in a cloying silence made thicker by the dense hedge boundaries. At the first choice of directions, they both paused.

"Which way now?"

Liv closed her eyes again then shook her head. "I can sense her in that direction, but who knows which way leads to the middle."

"Well, there's a trick to mazes…If you put a hand to the wall and keep that hand connected, you'll eventually get to the centre or the other side. It's not the most direct route, but it works."

"Worth a try." Liv reached out and touched the small leaves of the nearest hedge wall. "Ahhh!"

Mort copied her, the cool leaves parting under his touch and then a sharp thorn pressed into the pad of his thumb. He shook his hand and sucked the wound.

He let Liv lead, the hedge melting away at her touch as she manipulated the dream. The maze became darker as they headed deeper into its twists and turns. Mort glanced up at the sky. Swirling red and black clouds formed a spiral over the centre of the maze, and that couldn't be good. Liv picked up the pace and Mort scurried behind.

A scream cut through the deep silence. Liv stopped in her tracks and looked back at Mort.

"That's not good." Mort stated the obvious.

Liv looked from her hand to the hedge wall. "Screw this," she muttered. She waved her hands at the hedge in the direction of the scream and the tempest still circling overhead. The plant withered away until a square hole formed, large enough for them to squeeze through.

"You couldn't have done that before?"

Liv pierced Mort with a glare. "It's not the best idea to mess with dreams until you're sure of the cause." Another scream split the air. "But, in this case, I'd say it's an emergency. Come on!"

Liv repeated her manipulation of the dream until they were one hedge away from the centre. Here, they could hear scuffles and the sizzle of magic. A fight.

They looked at each other. Mort walked back to the last bushy wall and wrenched a branch out of the dense hedge. He held it like a bat and nodded to Liv.

Liv raised her hands and forced the final hedge to part. They darted through. The centre of the maze had no opening to the rest of the labyrinth and Mort twisted as he heard the hedge regrowing behind them.

Two witches stood facing each other. Both panted heavily from exhaustion. Scattered shards of ceramic lay on the ground near stone pillars that had previously held busts from ancient mythology. Mort recognised a curly beard on a Zeus head among the squashed tulips and ornamental roses that were the remains of flowerbeds. As they watched, one of the witches let out a beam of light at the other.

With a movement too fast to follow, the second witch cast a shield, and the light reflected laser sharp through one of the remaining rose bushes and towards Mort and Liv. They dived and hit the sandy floor as the beam arced overhead. The ray singed the dark hedge that had reformed behind them. The stench of burning shrubbery filled the air, along with a hiss of smoke.

With a scream of frustration, the first witch lowered her hands, and the light disappeared. Mort brushed sand off his face and stared. One of the witches was Effie, the elderly lady who ran the café, but who was the other?

The older woman glared at Effie with a passionate hatred that threatened to incinerate the entire garden. Mort braced himself against it. He'd faced worse.

Effie raised her arms and directed her power at the unfamiliar witch. The witch wasn't as quick with a shield as Effie and instead dodged behind a half-destroyed statue that now only showed a muscled torso and one perfect anatomically correct leg. The torso shattered under the blast. A shower of stone chinked to the ground and Mort ducked, covering his head.

The witch laughed bitterly. "You really think you can kill me? This ended days ago; you were just too stupid to know it!"

From the diminished cover of the statue, she loosed off another stream of light. Neither of them had noticed the two interlopers watching from the ground.

Liv crawled over to Mort. "We have to stop them before one of them kills the other. I've got a feeling it will be more permanent than in normal dreams."

Mort nodded.

"You take her, and I'll grab Effie. And don't get yourself killed!" With that, she took off towards Effie, staying close to the maze wall. Mort mirrored her from the other side, blending into the dark shadows around the edge like he was born to it. Sometimes he was glad of his birth right.

He kept the witch in his sight, creeping closer. A familiar weight settled at his waist as the sword of Arawn materialised at his side. Mort looked down. He supposed it made sense that the god of death's blade could follow him between realms, but he hadn't expected it.

With a surge of confidence that came from knowing he had a blade that could cut through anything, he rugby tackled the unfamiliar witch. His school P.E teacher would have been proud at his expert tackle as the witch fell to the ground with a shriek and a thump, her attack blasting harmlessly over Effie's head.

She twisted in his grasp, kicking up dust from the sandy ground. He cried out as she slammed a stick into his shoulder. Mort wrenched the branch from her and she let out a strangled cry, choked off by the dust in the air. He threw the weapon into the thick hedge before shifting his weight and digging his knees into the witch's arms, pinning her hands to the ground with his heavier body.

A scuffle sounded from the other side of the clearing.

"Have you got her?" Liv's voice floated over the roses.

"Yes!"

"OK, hang on."

With a shimmer that sent a burst of nausea through Mort's stomach, the hedge maze disappeared, along with the red clouded sky. The witch rippled beneath him and was gone.

"What the –?" He turned his head, searching for her, and there she was, tied to a chair, as if nothing had ever happened. The restrained witch glared at them, rocking against her bindings, trying to find a way out.

Mort pushed himself to his feet, clutching his bruised shoulder – why did things still hurt in a dream? – and moved to Liv's side, trying to hide the awe from his face. She had done all that with a thought.

The dream witch tilted her head at him, her eyes on his shoulder.

"She hit me with the stick," he said sheepishly in answer to Liv's unspoken question. "Couldn't you have tied them up like this in the first place?"

"That's not how it works. With those emotions flying around, there was no way to control the dream." She turned back to the two captured witches. "OK, someone tell us what is going on."

Chapter 33

"Thank goodness you're here! This crazy witch is trying to kill me!"

"Pah! If you think they'll believe that, then you're stupider than I thought," Effie spat out and looked away from the other witch as if she were disgusted by her.

Mort frowned at the two restrained witches. There was something strange here. Something tugged at his mind as he stared at them. Effie looked younger, and he knew a lot of patients who would pay good money for the skin treatment her dream self had, but she was still wearing a sequinned cardigan, almost as glamourous as that ridiculous outfit she'd donned for the reading. At least she wasn't wearing the turban.

The other witch glared at Effie. She appeared to be a similar age to the older magic user. She wore a well-cut dress that hugged her slim body oddly, as if it were designed for someone much younger.

"Who are you?" Liv looked at the unfamiliar witch.

"Hear that Riri? They don't recognise you; you can't hide yourself in this place."

If looks could kill, Effie wouldn't have a chance. As it was, the nonagenarian continued to breathe in the dream realm and managed to look even more disdainful, if that were possible.

"I am Adriana," the old woman spoke through clenched teeth, biting out each word.

"My sister," added Effie with a long-suffering sigh.

And suddenly, the similarities between the two women became more pronounced. The same long noses. The slightly rounded eyes. Even their dimpled chins were the same.

"Adriana?" Liv's voice was thick with disbelief.

The ping in Mort's subconscious sounded louder and he pursed his lips as he tried to focus.

The witch let out a hoarse laugh. "It was as much a shock to see me like this as it is for you. But who can understand how dreams work? Now I really need to get back. Can you help me?"

"You can't get back yourself?" Liv asked.

"I've never had a problem before, but then she showed up and now she's captured me here somehow! Please, you have to help!"

"Why don't you tell them why I 'showed up' Riri? I'm sure they'd be interested in hearing all about that."

Adriana narrowed her eyes and clamped her lips shut.

196

"Alright, I'll tell them. My sister managed to track me down after decades of peace and quiet. Then she killed me when I wouldn't give her what she wanted, what our mother had entrusted to me to keep safe. And since then I've been trapped in her body with her."

"See! She's crazy! How could I be her sister?!"

Liv frowned.

"She masqueraded as my great-niece, of course. Her youth would be difficult to explain, given she's only two years my junior!"

"That's ridiculous!"

Mort's face screwed up as he tried to figure out who, if anyone, was telling the truth. They would only have one shot to get the right soul back into the body and his instincts screamed that something was wrong.

"So, Effie, you were murdered?" he asked.

"That's what I've been telling you!"

Mort turned to Liv. "If Effie was killed, that might explain why her spirit wouldn't go on to rest, but she shouldn't be here. I'm sorry Effie…"

Effie sighed. "Well, I can't say I wasn't expecting to go sooner or later…I have to admit, though, I wish I could have done more with my life."

"You heard her; she wants to go. Now get me back to my body!" Adriana wailed.

Liv looked between both witches again, before shaking her head. "It doesn't seem right…"

Mort sighed. "Death isn't always right but it is, for the most part, final."

"But she killed Effie."

"But Effie died. Adriana didn't…"

Liv took a couple of deep breaths and when she spoke again, her voice was calm. "Alright, sorry Effie."

"Wait!" Effie looked Liv in the eye. "Ask Agatha to look after the bees for me, Nell's too busy and they need a good garden to live in. Alright, now I'm ready."

Liv nodded, jutted out her chin and raised her hand towards Adriana.

"Wait!" Mort grabbed her arm and cocked his head to one side. Now he recognised the swirling alarm within him. The realm of death called. "There's something else." Mort closed his eyes, focusing on his link to the other world.

Chapter 34

The calm garden scene around them dissolved slowly, replaced by a large door that seemed to be made of stars. It rippled against the black sky. The witches in the chairs gaped with near matching expressions. Adriana strained against the bindings, trying to edge away from the door.

"Impressive. I can never get to the door between the veil that quickly," Liv said, appraising the doorway.

Mort looked around. "Is that what this is?"

Liv frowned. "You've never been here before? I thought your family helped the god of death?"

"We've got our own entrance to the other realm," he muttered. Liv took the hint. Now was not the time to press him on that.

Liv hesitated a moment, a strange longing passed over her face, but it disappeared, and she reached for the door. She motioned to Mort with her head, and he placed his own palm next to hers. The door of starlight deepened and stretched as it transformed into an archway between the planes of life and death. They crossed the threshold.

He heard Liv breathing deeply at his side. Of course, she wouldn't be used to travelling beyond the veil between life and death, but to him, it was as easy as slipping on a coat, a familiar power that sank into him, wrapping him in its warm embrace. Something in his bones, as his father would say. He smiled at her, trying to ease her fears.

"Welcome to Annwn, the other realm."

Somehow, in this realm, he grew more sure of himself. His t-shirt billowed as if caught in a breeze. Liv involuntarily took a step backwards from him, her eyes wide. He knew that look. He had worn it himself the first time his father had taken him through the portal and he had seen his dad change, becoming taller, becoming more, even as strange shadows darkened his face and his eyes burned with a bright light.

It had scared him at the time, but now the power was second nature, and people got scared of him. But they didn't have time. He peered into the darkness before striding forwards.

"Wait! It's not safe for us to wander in here. If we get lost, we might never get back." Liv trotted after him, looking over her shoulder at the archway that marked their exit.

"We won't get lost." He never got lost in the other realm. "Come on, it's this way."

"What are we looking for?" Liv asked, but Mort had moved further ahead.

They walked for an age, but the scenery never changed. A dull blue sky shimmered overhead, so dim it almost seemed grey, and silvery light lit the empty wasteland. Every so often a dark shade would appear on the edge of Mort's vision, but he ignored them, knowing that they would run if he tried to focus on them.

They continued along the pebbled ground until it gave way to rolling fields of golden grass. Liv stopped behind him as the scenery morphed, now full of vibrant trees and flowers. A bright phoenix flew overhead, lighting the sky with its flaming tail. He kept going, singular in his purpose as the dead called to him. He heard her scurry after him. And then they were there. He stopped and stumbled as Liv walked into his back.

"Sorry, there was a bird..." she mumbled

"There," he whispered, ignoring her apologies.

A pale shade sat with other figures in a small clearing by a river that shimmered like mercury. Mort walked over slowly, careful not to startle them. One of the spirits laughed at something. Another twined a daisy into a long line of flowers and hung it on a third shade's head.

Mort's shadow fell over them. The spirits stopped talking and stood, looking around nervously.

"There's no need to worry, I just want to talk." Mort kept his voice gentle, slipping easily into the tone he used for talking to children at his GP practice. A name slipped into his mind. "Is...Polly here?"

One of the figures raised her hand. She didn't meet Mort's eyes and instead stared at her bare feet. Mort gestured for her to follow them to the edge of the clearing, away from the others who clustered together and stared with large, round eyes from the opposite side.

"Polly, tell me who did this to you."

The girl studied her toes and shook her head. Liv tilted her head to one side.

"You won't get into trouble. Tell me and I can make this right."

Her eyes brimmed with unshed tears as she shook her head again, making her shoulder-length hair wave across her face.

Liv touched Mort softly on the arm and nudged him to one side before she took his place. He nodded and let her take the lead, maybe the spirit would feel more comfortable talking to a woman. Liv sat down near a tall, shady tree and patted the grass next to her. The young spirit sat silently, hugging her knees.

"Hi, Polly, is it?"

The girl nodded, her eyes landing on Liv's face before skittering away. "I'm Liv. We're here because something happened. Something bad." Mort settled against a tree a few feet away, close enough to hear everything, and listened as Liv's voice soothed the spirit. "But we want to help. What do you want Polly?"

This time, Polly met her gaze. "I want to stay here." Her voice was soft, but sure.

Mort frowned but stayed silent. Something about the spirit seemed familiar, but he couldn't place what it was.

"OK, why don't you talk me through what happened, and we'll take it from there."

The woman looked up at the swaying canopy of the tree, then down at her feet, then at a long blade of grass. She reached for the grass and twisted it absent-mindedly.

"I was killed. It took me a while to realise it, but I was in a hotel room one moment, then in a dark place with all these little stones on the floor. Then I sort of knew I had to walk and after a while, I found these fields and all these other women like me." For the first time since seeing Mort, the twenty-year-old ghost smiled.

"Tell me more about before you...transitioned to this place."

"Died, you mean?"

"Yes."

"Well, I don't know when it was exactly. Time doesn't seem to pass the same way here, but I remember it was cold, but she didn't wear gloves. A stupid thing to remember, but that's what struck me about her. I was shivering on the streets and this woman didn't even have to worry about remembering her gloves, she was so sure she'd be going somewhere warm."

"Who?"

"The lady who killed me. I mean, I didn't realise she was going to kill me. I thought she was trying to help. Do-gooder women tried to help sometimes when they saw me on the streets. I thought she was one of them. And she took me to a hotel and, fair play, I suppose, she did get me a burger, but then she killed me. It was weird, though…"

Liv nodded but stayed silent. Mort recognised the therapist's trick to keep others talking.

"I mean, I always expected dying to hurt, but she just said some words and then it was like I wasn't in my body anymore. I sort of floated above it. But the weirdest thing was that as I was looking down, my body moved and got up and her body just lay there like she had died. But she hadn't. She was in my body."

Mort blinked. Adriana had used this young lady's body. That was why he thought she looked familiar, he had seen this body walking and talking in the real world. He pushed himself of the tree trunk. This could not stand.

Liv glanced at Mort and he paused, respecting her experience as the therapist probed for more details. "And can you tell us what she looked like?"

"I can do better than that." Polly looked over at the group of women and called one of them over. "She was in Jenny's body." Liv stood as Jenny approached and Polly kept going. "Only I didn't know that then, of course, and she looked older than Jenny does."

Mort stepped forward. "So, this woman took your body, Jenny, then left it and took yours, Polly?"

Both women nodded. He stared into the middle distance for a long minute, listening as the realm of the dead confirmed what he'd suspected. He rubbed his forehead and

204

turned back to face them; his eyes tinged with sadness. There was nothing he could do for Jenny.

"I'm sorry, both of you, that you died before your time. Jenny, it's been too long to return you to your body. All I can offer you is an eternity here in Elysia, or a drink from the river of forgetfulness where you can be reborn."

"I'm happy here." Jenny's voice sounded musical, and she danced away to join the other women gathered across the glade.

He turned to face the newer spirit and reached for her hand. "Polly, if you come with me, I can return you to your body. A few months have passed, but you should be able to return to your life."

"No! I don't want to! You can't make me! Don't make me!" Polly clutched at Liv.

"You don't want to go back?"

"No! My life was horrible. I ran away from the bastard who beat me, but I was living on the streets, always afraid that he would find me and drag me back. I want to stay here. I'm happy here with Jenny and the others."

Liv looked at Mort and gestured with her eyes as Polly burst into tears. "I'm sure we can work something out."

The wrinkles on his forehead deepened. This girl was difficult. He forced his lips to stay straight as the face of another difficult woman floated into his mind. Fiona. He could imagine her frown now, how simple she would find this, how she would want the right thing to be done. "Well, of course you can stay here if you desire…"

205

"Yes! Yes, that is what I desire. Thank you! Thank you!" Impulsively, Polly threw her arms around Liv, then Mort, and skipped back to join the others.

"What are we going to do now?"

Chapter 35

Mort shook his head. "No idea," he lied, because he had a plan. One that went against everything he'd been taught about fate and the lines that shouldn't be crossed.

"We can't give Adriana back Polly's body!"

"Obviously not. But…"

"But what?"

Mort sighed as he worked it through. "People have an allotted time woven by the Fates." He raised his hands to forestall Liv's protest. "It's not fair, but it is what it is. Polly should still be alive. So should Jenny, by rights."

"But their fates have been changed."

Mort nodded, his face grim.

"So why don't we change some fates of our own?"

There. She'd spoken the words he couldn't bring himself to. He could do it. Theoretically. He'd never gone against fate before, never turned back the clock and allowed a spirit to leave the other realm, but then, he'd never been faced with this sort of injustice. Murders, yes. Demons, for sure. But this… He nodded. He would face Arawn and explain himself if needed, but maybe the god wouldn't even notice…

He didn't say a word as he led the way back to the gateway between the realms. It was amazing how he could lie to himself that everything would be alright, that there would be no consequences for messing with fate. Too late now, though. There was only one right course of action. Only one way he could meet Fi's clear gaze when they returned.

Once they stepped back into the dream realm, Liv turned to Mort and nodded. He placed a hand on the sword at his side, taking comfort from the cold metal hilt.

The two women were still tied to their padded chairs exactly where Liv had left them. Adriana's eyes widened as they returned, her hair was wild where she had thrashed against the psychic bindings. Effie sat resolutely still.

"You're a murderer." Mort didn't sugarcoat it.

"What? What are you talking about? Effie, what are they talking about?"

Effie stared at her sister. "Oh Riri, what did you do?"

Adriana rolled her eyes when she realised no one was buying her act. "Come on, what did you think when I showed up? That I'd manage to reverse age?"

"I thought you must have found a spell…or that stupid fountain of youth you were obsessed by, but…you killed someone?"

"Two someones, at least," Liv added, her eyes on Adriana.

"I did them a favour! You should have seen the state of them. I only went for the down and outs on the street. They had nothing to live for, so I freed them. You've come back alone, so I take it she didn't want to come back? I thought not. Anyway, it's all your fault!" Adriana spat at Effie. "I wouldn't have had to change my body if you'd have just given me the crystal in the first place instead of running away. All I wanted was eternal youth! I had the potential to do so much good in the world, if I only had more time. But you couldn't let me have it, could you? Grandmother's favourite little goody two shoes. Pah." She spat again. "Well, I found another way to be young."

"So, what do you want the crystal for if you're happy killing innocent young women so you can keep a wrinkle-free face?"

A twisted smile crept onto Adriana's face. "The soul transference only works so many times. The girl I killed last year was my last chance and I've got so much I want to do, besides, just think what the crystal can give me! How much good I could do? I only have to desire something, and I'll see it, know how to get it. Not only eternal youth but anything... I could change the world, make it better for our kind. Wouldn't you kill for something like that?"

Effie shook her head sadly. "No. No, I wouldn't. I've worked for what I have. I should have made sure you learned that lesson."

"Goody two shoes Effie. It doesn't matter, anyway. You're dead and my new body is still down there. Now untie these ropes and get me back where I belong!"

Mort stepped forward. He drew his large silver sword and gripped the leather hilt. White runes swirled over the blade. When he spoke, his voice held an echo of another power behind it.

"You asked to go where you belong, Adriana. Let me tell you where that is. The afterlife can be a joyous place filled with everlasting peace and love, but for evil doers there is an alternative. It is not a peaceful place, and it is not kind or forgiving. It is a realm of self-made torment, warped by the inhabitants. And that is where you will go to lament your choices and see if you can learn from your awful mistakes."

"But...but...you can't!"

"On behalf of Arawn, God of Death, I can, and I will." He twirled the sword in his hand.

***

Adriana's eyes widened with fear. She pleaded, then screwed her eyes shut, expecting pain as the point of the sword came closer. When she felt nothing more than a slight pressure on her forehead, she opened her eyes in triumph before squinting in confusion. She was free from her bonds, but she was in another, more terrifying realm entirely.

***

Liv walked round the empty chair. "Has she really gone to hell?"

Mort winced at the word. "It is a place of punishment, yes." Liv pursed her lips and Mort continued. "Would you have evil deeds go unpunished?"

She thought for a moment then shook her head, folding her arms around her body. She shuddered, then he sensed a change, as if she'd shuttered her thoughts away.

"OK, so what happens now? Adriana's, I mean Polly's, body is still in the hospital."

"Well, if there's a spare body going, I wouldn't mind going back…"

Mort looked from Effie to Liv, then back to Effie. With a small sigh, he snapped his fingers.

Chapter 36

Fi's eyes flicked from the two prone bodies on the floor to the patient in the hospital bed. Agatha paced nervously. The space available for pacing was tiny as, although it was a private room, it was still in a hospital. Periodically, she checked on the containment spells she had set up, adding to them when she felt a power spike.

"It'll be alright, you know," Agatha reassured her younger sister.

Fi snorted. "You don't know that."

"No, but in my experience, everything always turns out alright in the end."

Fi rolled her eyes. "How can you say that, even after…"

"After what?" Agatha narrowed her eyes.

"Never mind."

Long minutes of silence stretched between them. "I know what you were going to say." Agatha's voice was barely above a whisper as she busied herself by smoothing down the baby blue blanket on the bed.

Fi focused on her sister. "I didn't mean…"

"You're right, it was a really crap time going through miscarriage after miscarriage, but you know what? The bad times drew me and Neville closer together. And then Bea came along…the light of my life. She's an absolute joy and I wouldn't trade her for anything. I don't know why I expect you to understand."

Fi stood slowly, breathing through the pain that bloomed in her chest. If her sister was swearing, even a mild curse word like crap, she was really upset. She shuffled towards Agatha and pulled her into a loose, sideways hug. "I'm sorry Aggy, I really am."

Agatha returned the hug for a few seconds before a small squeal exited her mouth. Fi pulled back and studied her sister. Agatha's eyes were on the floor behind Fi's back.

"Look, they're back!"

Fi leaned on the bed and watched as first Liv, then Mort opened their eyes and stood. Liv was upright almost immediately, but Mort took a few moments to get his bearings before he staggered up woozily.

"How did it go?" Fi demanded.

"What are you doing standing?" Mort frowned at the injured witch and moved to help her back into the chair.

Fi shrugged him off and instead turned to face the bed. The four supernaturals crowded round, leaning forward, waiting for Adriana's eyes to open. Nothing happened. Mort stepped forward to study the machines attached to the patient.

"She's stable and there's only one soul available now…" He turned from the machine and bent over the patient to lift one of Adriana's eyelids.

"What does that mean?"

He took out his pocket torch and shone it directly into her eyes. "No response."

He shared a look with Liv.

Fi crossed her arms. "What happened?"

Liv's full mouth turned down. "Turns out you were right; Adriana was a killer, but Effie wasn't her first. This body belonged to a young woman, the latest in a series of murders so Adriana could stay young. She wasn't Effie's great-niece either, she was her sister."

"So, we've just helped a murderer back to her body?!"

"Not quite. Mort, uh, sentenced Adriana to hell and the previous owner didn't want her body back, so I'm hoping that Effie is in there somewhere."

"Then we've got to wake her!"

"A shock might do it. If I can get a defibrillator in here, the shock to her heart might kickstart her to consciousness." Mort stood up, allowing the eyelid to fall closed.

"Yes. Do that!"

"We need to hurry; I can feel her power spiking." Agatha hastily added more magic to the ward with staccato arm movements.

Mort hurried off to find the machine. Liv took up his place at the bedside, frowning slightly.

"What is it?" Agatha asked between motions.

"There's always the chance that Effie's consciousness is rejecting its new body. After all, she's had over ninety years in her previous one. It'll be a shock to suddenly be in her twenties again…"

"Then we should hurry. Where's the doctor?" Fi shambled to the door and peeked through the pane of glass. The lights flickered on and off. "What was that?"

Agatha shook her head and redoubled her wild waving as she reworked the spell. "That's the power spike, it's starting to surge!"

The floor trembled. A nanosecond later, the lights went out. The door opened. The three women shrieked as a dark figure loomed in the doorway.

"Sorry, just me." Mort sidled into the room past Fi. "Power's out and for some reason, the back-up generator isn't kicking in, so a defibrillator won't work. I brought the kit, but without a power supply, it's useless."

"It's the unstable magic." Agatha was frantic now.

"We need to wake her!"

"Not us. You." Mort gripped Fi's hand gently but firmly.

"What?" Fi gaped at him, then at the body on the bed.

"You." Mort nodded, his voice oozing confidence. "You can control electricity, right? That's all a defibrillator does;

it puts a small current into the body to shock the heart. You can do this."

Fi sank against the wall and shook her head. "No, no, I can't."

Agatha looked around anxiously. "Her power is spiking; I don't think the wards will hold much longer. You can do it, Fi! You have to or we're all dead."

"I can't!" Fi wailed, her voice high and panicked. She tried to find her sister's face in the semi-darkness. "What if I lose control again and kill her? You've seen what I can do! I hurt Mum and I...I killed that beekeeper!"

Agatha left the wards and hugged her little sister. "You were a child when you hurt Mum and it was an accident. We all know that. And the beekeeper tried to kill us! It was self-defence and besides, you didn't do that by yourself, you know, if anyone's to blame, it's me and my magic."

"No..." Tears spilled down Fi's face.

"No one's going to force you, but if you don't try, then we'll definitely lose Effie and a lot more people when the room explodes." Agatha used the calm and patient tones she practiced daily in the classroom.

The bluntness of Agatha's words caught Fi in the chest. There was a chance to save Effie and use her power to protect people instead of hurting them. And really, she didn't have a choice. If she didn't channel her magic, then they would all die. Her sister, her friends and her...well who knew what exactly Mort's relationship with her was, but she was sure she wanted him alive. Fi sniffed, then nodded once. She turned to Mort. "Tell me what I have to do."

Mort led her to the bed and opened the hospital gown over the patient's chest. "You place your palms here and here." He placed gel pads on the spots he indicated. "Now you don't want to overdo it, but too little won't have the effect we're looking for. Anywhere between two hundred and a thousand volts should do it."

Fi's head reeled. "What does that mean? How much power do you want? Like a lightning bolt?"

"No!" Mort adjusted his voice. "No, not a lightning bolt. Just a bit more than mains electricity. Got it?"

Fi nodded. She closed her eyes and allowed herself to feel her power. Always ready, it prickled easily under her skin and her hair frizzed out in a static halo. She willed her magic to her palms, adjusting the level until she thought it was about right, judging it as slightly more than when she shorted out a computer.

"OK, when I say 'go', give me a brief burst of your power. Ready? Go!"

At Mort's urging, she released a surge of electricity through her palms. Adriana's body jolted up slightly and her hair fanned out in response to the charge, but her eyes stayed closed.

"OK, a little more power. Ready? Go!"

Fi coaxed more energy into her electricity and let loose another burst of power. Her white-blonde hair frizzed until it stood out from her head, as her magic crackled through her body. The witch in the bed jerked off the sheets. A flash of light pulsed from her body as the witch's power surged out of her in a beam that burned into the ceiling. Fi screwed her eyes shut and tensed for impact. When nothing happened, she risked looking down at the bed.

The patient's eyes flew open and Adriana, or possibly Effie, looked around.

Chapter 37

"Would anyone care to tell me what is going on?" The witch on the bed asked, taking in the four interlopers in her room. As her gaze swept past their faces, her eyes landed on her chest. "Sweet hells, what is this?" Careless of the observers, she ran her hands up her youthful body and let out a soft whistle.

"Effie?"

The witch's grey eyes snapped up. She speared Liv and then Mort with her piercing gaze. "It worked then? I thought it was a dream... Thank you."

Mort nodded, then coughed. "Medically speaking, I'd say you're a fit and healthy young woman. I think we'd better leave you to have some privacy..."

Effie half-heartedly pulled the covers over her exposed chest and chuckled. The rich laugh sounded far too old and worldly for the body she now inhabited.

Agatha gave the woman a hug before ushering her exhausted sister from the room and back up to her own hospital bed.

A few days later…

Fi stretched out on the sofa in the fancy drawing room. Her mother pretended she hadn't winced at Fi's feet on the upholstery and fussed with the teapot. Fi smiled, enjoying the indulgence of being waited on. Cressida curled up on her lap and snuck biscuits from the china plate as often as she could. Effie sat across from her on a mock renaissance blue velvet chair that would have looked at home in a French chateau. She looked comfortable in her new body, although she moaned about the clothes Adriana had left her and was determined to 'fill out the curves' as she put it.

Effie lifted another bite of cake to her mouth. "But I still can't understand how you knew to come to the shop at just the right time to catch Adriana rooting through the rubble."

"I saw it in the crystal."

That makes sense.

"It does?" Fi stared at Cressida.

The wyrm flicked its forked tongue out. *It shows you what you desire, yes?*

Fi nodded.

And you've been obsessing over Effie's death. It's only natural the crystal would show you her killer.

220

Fi tapped her fingers on the sofa and relayed Cressida's theory to the others.

"I still can't believe Adriana killed Effie, I mean, you."

Effie shrugged. "It was fate, I suppose. I had what she wanted, and she was never one to take no for an answer. The crystal ball belonged to my grandmother, a powerful seer in her own right. She had her own stage show back when Queen Victoria was alive, even read for the Queen herself if the rumours were true. She saw the defects in my sister's character from a young age and warned my mother. But mother and I were blinded by our love for her. When grandmama was on her deathbed, she left me the crystal I gave to you with instructions to keep it from Adriana.

"To Adriana, she gave a purse of money and her own standard crystal ball. It wasn't enough. She found out that I had inherited a greater prize and tried to take it from me. But I had hidden it well. She tortured me, nearly killed me to get it. Mother found us just in time and stopped her. She cursed Adriana so she could never enter our family home. But it became too dangerous to stay. Adriana was always there, waiting, biding her time. She was obsessed with the crystal. She thought it could give her eternal youth and endless power…" Effie shuddered at the memory of her sister.

"Mother became ill, her heart broken because of the actions of her daughter. She died shortly afterwards. I was protected by the curse but trapped because of it too. So, one day, I ran. It was easier to lose yourself in those days. I travelled across the world, running and trying to stay ahead of my sister. Until I found a sanctuary of sorts. Omensford is a protected space for magic users. There are so many of us here. I hid in plain sight, told everyone to call me Effie, and my real name was practically forgotten.

"I got complacent, I suppose, because she found me. It took her decades, but she found me. And when I wouldn't tell her where the crystal was, she killed me and burned the body. She was smart, she made it look like an accident. But now she's gone and the crystal's safe from her schemes."

"Speaking of…" Fi rummaged in her pocket and held out the small crystal ball to the witch. "This belongs to you."

Effie picked up the crystal ball and stared into its purplish depths. "Maybe this thing has too much power…maybe mortals shouldn't see how to achieve their desires so easily, after all, people can achieve most things through hard work and perseverance with a tinge of inspiration…maybe it's too dangerous to have around." Her fingers gripped it tightly, before hurling it against the floor. Shards scattered over the parquet.

Nell blinked at the sudden mess in her drawing room. "Was that really necessary?"

Fi gaped.

"I should have done that years ago." Effie rolled her shoulders back, a broad smile filling her face.

"What are you going to do now?" Nell asked, before taking a sip of her scalding hot tea as she toed aside a large piece of crystal.

Effie tapped her cheek thoughtfully with the silver cake fork. "Well, I suppose it would be nice to travel again…"

Fi's phone rang as Effie began listing places she'd like to visit. She struggled off the sofa and into the hallway as she answered.

"Hello?"

"Hello, is that Fiona Blair?"

"Speaking. And look, if this is someone trying to sell me personal protection insurance…"

"No, no, it's Joel, Joel Minchin from GlobalCorpIT."

"Oh, right, hi," Fi internally told herself to stop speaking, she sounded like a moron.

"I'm calling you to say that we didn't think you were the right fit for the consultant vacancy…"

Fi forced herself to take a deep breath. "Why would you think that?"

"We felt that someone of your experience wouldn't be happy in a standard consulting role…"

"I would, honestly, I'd be fine in that role. If it was finding that virus, then I'm sorry, but…"

"If you let me finish Ms Blair, I understand you're disappointed, but I'm calling to offer you a team leader role."

"Team leader?"

"Yes, you'll be responsible for a team of twenty consultants. It should be fairly straightforward. They'll handle the calls, and you can train them up, offer support and guidance and of course you'll be on hand for those really tricky problems where switching it on and off again just won't cut it." Joel laughed at his own joke.

"Right…"

"I realise this is a lot to take in, so I've emailed over the contract and the job description. It's all fairly standard, but if you have any questions at all, you can call me. My number's in the email."

"OK, thank you," Fi stammered.

"Not at all, thank you. I'll let you think it over but don't take too long." With a final burst of weak laughter, Joel hung up.

Fi removed her phone from her ear and stared at it. Nell opened the door to the drawing room curiously and looked at her shocked daughter. She rushed over and helped Fi back to the sofa.

"Are you alright? What's happened?"

Fi looked up blankly. "I think I've just been offered a job."

"That's brilliant news! At the tech firm? The job you wanted? Did you hear that, Effie? Fi's got a job at last!"

"I'm sitting right here and I'm not as deaf as I used to be! Congratulations, Fi!"

Fi nodded while her mother pulled out champagne glasses and bustled to the kitchen to retrieve a bottle of prosecco that she always kept on ice in case of emergency celebrations. Nell never wanted to be unprepared.

As the three witches toasted her new job and Effie's new life, Fi wondered why her heart felt like it had plummeted through the floor and her chest was gripped with a dull ache that made her feel caged.

Chapter 38

Nell tapped the microphone once, twice, then a third time. The Omensford residents winced at the hard sound reverberating through the speakers set up in the village hall.

"Good afternoon, everyone, it is my absolute pleasure to welcome you to the Ophelia Harrington Spring Social! The organising committee has really outdone themselves this year. Refreshments are available from the kitchen and I'm reliably informed that she has passed her recipe for thick cut marmalade on to her great-niece who has whipped up a batch in memory of our beloved friend, Effie." Nell paused for the applause that followed and she winked at Effie, who was still carrying on the pretence of being her own great-niece. Effie curtseyed gracefully in her flat shoes and returned the wink.

"There is, of course, the annual tombola run by the WWWI, always open to new members. This year the top prize is a cream tea at the Pump Rooms in Bath. Other prizes include a night at my own Bed and Breakfast and a hamper of local Cotswolds produce, kindly provided by the many talented artisans in our local community. And Sita has asked me to announce that the photo booth is open, and she has a wide variety of filters and backgrounds available for a small donation to charity, which, in honour of Effie will be split between the Cotswolds Fire Department and her beloved Witches', Wizards' and Warlocks' Institute." Nell consulted the notecard in her hand. "Finally, thanks to an enormous number of generous donations, the bottle raffle is up to two tables! Get in early for your chance to win a bottle of champagne or some luxury bubble bath. And now, please welcome to the stage, the Hoe-down Hobgoblins, who will lead us in our barn dance before Jeremy Vinyl rounds off the evening with his DJ set."

More applause accompanied the band, who had dressed in checked shirts and denim dungarees for the occasion. The lead singer chewed a long stem of hay and grinned at the crowd before calling out the first dance moves.

Fi wound her way through the throng of dancers to Effie's side. "You're not running the refreshment stand this year, then?"

"I thought I'd take a break, after all, I've been doing it for the last forty years!"

"Have you thought any more about what you might do now you're not…"

"Old?"

"I was going to say 'in hiding'!"

Effie smiled, her grey eyes twinkling. "Yes, I've made up my mind. Agatha's agreed to look after my bees, so I'm going to go travelling again. I've booked a cruise with some of the insurance money. Adriana had quite a bit of money squirrelled away in savings accounts, and I intend to spend it! I feel like I've got a whole new life to live!"

A young farmer interrupted and asked Effie for a dance. She gave a throaty laugh and accepted. Fi sipped her diet coke and smiled as she watched the couple spin across the floor in time to the rhythmic country style music.

"Are you going back into the tech industry then?" Liv appeared at her side, a gin and tonic in her hand.

Fi sighed. News travelled fast in the small village. "I guess...it's just..."

"You weren't feeling stimulated, fulfilled, or appreciated in your old job?"

Fi stared at her friend.

"And you're worried that this job will be the same."

"I thought therapists were just supposed to listen, not read minds."

Liv shrugged. "I'm not your therapist, I'm your friend, and it wasn't exactly a secret you were bored in tech support. Why would it be different in a new role?"

"The pay is better..."

"That's because they have to pay those salaries to get anyone to even consider doing the job!"

"I hadn't thought of it like that."

"All I'm saying is that sometimes when people are in a crisis period like you've been in since you lost your job, they can use that time to think about what they really want. It's why so many people resigned during Covid. They had enough time and space to think about things and realised they hated their jobs and could do something different."

Fi took a sip of her drink and contemplated her friend's words. It could be true. She hadn't enjoyed her old job, and she'd ignored the email that Joel had sent, leaving it marked as unread in her inbox since he'd called. "But what else can I do?"

"That's something only you can decide, unless you want to pay me five hundred pounds per hour to analyse your dreams."

"What about a friends and family discount?"

"That is my friends and family discount!"

"Wow, you have a lot of very rich clients."

Liv nodded.

"Maybe I should retrain as a therapist…"

Liv snorted. "I think you actually have to like people to be a therapist."

"I like people, just not as much as machines. And they want me to manage people! Ugh, I'm going to be stuck as a tech consultant forever."

"Maybe not, Ms Blair." A commanding voice sounded near Fi's ear. She jumped and spilled her drink down her lumberjack style shirt. The coke soaked into the absorbent material as she tried to mop it up. She turned. "Agent Jones! Maxi! What are you doing here?"

"Well, we didn't come for the Spring Social. A word?" The lynx shifter looked around the packed hall. "Outside?"

Without waiting for a reply, the tall woman strode across the dance floor and through the open double doors. Maxi gave her a look and gestured for her to follow with a small bow and a wink. Fi exchanged glances with Liv, then headed for the exit, following the path that Agent Jones had carved through the dancers.

In the warm evening air, Fi squinted until she saw Agent Jones standing apart from the people gathered outside, sitting on hay bales, and sipping cold cider. She felt her power start to tingle under her skin and tamped it down. She had nothing to be nervous about. She'd done nothing wrong. But Agent Jones' amber eyes made her feel like the officer knew all her secrets. She folded her arms as if that would create a barrier between them.

"I won't beat about the bush, Fiona; may I call you Fiona?"

"Fi, my friends call me Fi."

"Alright, well, I want to offer you a job. I've had glowing reports about you from Madam Mim about your work last Halloween on the Goody Winships case, Maxi sings your praises, and there's been a disturbance in the magical fields around Omensford recently. I've asked around and apparently you saved the day again." Her eyes narrowed. "Although no one will tell me exactly what happened..."

Fi kept quiet and forced herself to meet Agent Jones' hard stare. She wasn't sure what the Magical Liaison Office's stance was on soul transference, but she wasn't about to risk losing Effie to some sinister laboratory. The shifter tapped her foot on the ground impatiently.

"If you're going to work for me, you'll have to trust me…"

"And you'll have to trust me." From the approving look in Agent Jones' eyes, that was the right answer. "What exactly is the job?" Fi tried to keep the keenness from her voice.

"I want eyes and ears on the ground here. Omensford and its surroundings are a protected magical area. Recent restructures mean my area now includes the Southwest of England as well as Wales. I don't want to have to travel up here every few months because the local police can't deal with a bit of magic. So, I want you to be the Magical Liaison Office's community consultant here. You've got good instincts and problem-solving skills and, of course, you're a local. That counts for a lot in community work."

Fi's heart leapt. The shifter smiled slightly; her keen senses must have picked up Fi's excitement.

"If you're interested, I'll get Maxi to send through a contract. It won't pay as much as your tech job, but it'll be more exciting. I can guarantee it." She grinned wolfishly, and Fi found herself smiling back. The shifter nodded, her neat bob staying in place as her head moved. "Right, I'm going to get a drink before we head back. Maxi?"

"Yah, sure. Uh, Fi, can I have a word?" Maxi asked, pulling one hand through his hair, causing it to stick out in a mad professor style.

Agent Jones stalked off to find some refreshments while Maxi stood.

"Hi."

"Hi Maxi, good to see you again."

"Yah, you, too." He seemed relieved and barrelled on, speeding up as he became more excited, "I wanted to say that I've been working on something I think you're going to like. It's a battery that can store magical energy. I got the idea on a trip to the alps with Tristan. There was a storm, and we got so wasted on the French vino…but anyway, I thought of you and harnessing all your energy. I think it could be totally useful for your power. I mean, you've basically got free electricity on tap, yah?"

Fi's heart sank. "Maxi, can I ask you something?"

"Yah, of course you can Fifi."

"Are you interested in me or my power?"

His gaze moved from his shined shoes to Fi to the hay bales and back to Fi.

"I, uh, I just…"

"I think that answers my question. Thanks for thinking of me, you're a good friend Maxi. Let me know how you get on with the battery." With that, she walked back inside, leaving the youthful Magical Liaison Officer standing on the edge of the festivities.

Back inside, she headed straight for the refreshments stand. Diet cola just wasn't going to cut it tonight. She ordered a beer instead and took a large swig from the plastic pint glass.

"G'day, little lady."

Fi snorted and almost sprayed beer over Mort. "I think g'day is Australian!"

He swept his hand across the brim of his fancy dress cowboy hat and smiled. "Sorry partner."

She found herself returning his grin. "I hear the organising committee outdid themselves this year."

"Oh yes, what do you think of the bunting?"

"Very good. Really adds to the ambiance. Was that you?"

"It was all your mother would trust me with. Well, that and the signs."

"Great font choice."

"Thanks, I almost went with Comic Sans, but decided to stick with something more classic."

"I think it really works."

"So, you did promise to be my guide tonight…"

Fi pretended to think. "So, I did. What did you have in mind?"

"How about a dance?"

Fi downed the rest of her pint, left the cup on a windowsill and linked her arm through his. He led the way to the dancefloor, where Fi spotted Agatha and Neville doing a variation on square dancing as Effie and her new beau stamped in time to the music. With a devastating grin, Mort unlinked his arm from hers and they attempted to follow the calls that the lead hobgoblin shouted into the microphone.

Epilogue

Fi woke up the next morning with a headache. How many pints of slightly warm lager had she had last night? She groaned and rolled over in her bed. Except it wasn't her bed.

As she came to, she realised that the crisp white sheets were far softer than her own and didn't feature an embarrassing assortment of comic book characters more suited to a teenage boy than someone over thirty.

She finished her roll and felt warm skin touch hers. She backed away until she was on the very edge of the king-sized bed. She slipped one foot out from under the covers until it landed on a plush carpet. Once she was certain she wasn't going to fall, she forced the rest of herself out of the bed too. She crept to a door that she hoped was an ensuite.

The dark-haired figure in the bed started to move, so she opened the door and stepped in, closing it behind her. Too late, she realised it wasn't a shower room.

"Fi?"

She kept quiet.

"Fi, I just saw you go into the wardrobe. Do you want to borrow a shirt?"

Fi looked down. She wasn't naked, but she wasn't exactly comfortable in just her underwear, chosen more for its comfort than desire-producing properties. Did she even want to provoke desire? Her head hurt.

The door opened slowly. Fi panicked and grabbed the nearest item of clothing from a hanger.

"Just, uh, getting something to wear."

Mort nodded with a lopsided grin on his face. His dark hair flopped over his forehead, giving him an endearing just-got-out-of-bed look. She pushed past him and threw the t-shirt over her head.

"I just want to, uh, use the bathroom."

Mort nodded and gestured to another door. She scurried towards it. He leaned back on the built-in wardrobe and watched her go.

"I'll get some breakfast started, shall I?" he called after her.

She made a noise that could have meant 'yes' and clicked the bathroom door shut behind her. Once safely inside, she stared at her dishevelled form in the mirror. What had she done?

Thank you

A special thank you to my amazing patreon: Emma Ward who always supports me.

If you want to support Gemma, you can find her on patreon for exclusive first reads of new stories.

You can also join her newsletter for bonus chapters that show the dream sequence from Liv's point of view and a free short story about Liv – Case Notes of a Supernatural Sleep Therapist: The Demon

You can also get a free prequel to her Rise of Dragons series and follow Gemma on www.instagram.com/gemmaclatworthy, www.facebook.com/gemmaclatworthy or join the reader's group Gemma's book wyrms.

Other Books by G Clatworthy

Books in the Rise of the Dragons series:

Awakening

Solstice of Dragons

Equinox Betrayal

Darkest Deception

Attack on Avalon

Fated Bloodlines

Books in the Omensford series (set in the Rise of Dragons universe):

Bedsocks and Broomsticks

Cream Teas and Crystal Balls

Donkeys and Demons

Children's Books

The Child Who series:

<u>The Girl Who Lost Her Listening Ears</u>

<u>The Boy Who Lost His Listening Ears</u>

<u>The Girl Who Dreamed of Sleep</u>

<u>The Boy Who Dreamed of Sleep</u>

Nanny Pastry series:

<u>Nanny Pastry and the Nimble Ninjabread Man</u>

Other books:

<u>Coronavirus in the words of children</u>

About the Author

Gemma started writing during the 2020 lockdown and loves fantasy fiction and dragons in particular. She lives in Wiltshire with her family and two cats and also enjoys crafts of all kinds. You can see all her writing on patreon. Join the conversation at Gemma's book wyrms readers' group on Facebook.

She also writes children's books. You can find out more on her website www.gemmaclatworthy.com or follow her on Instagram (www.instagram.com/gemmaclatworthy) or Facebook (www.facebook.com/gemmaclatworthy).